Forging the Shilling Girl

EMMA HARDWICK

Drina
ROMANCE
PUBLISHING

COPYRIGHT

Title: Forging the Shilling Girl

Print version published in 2021

Copyright © 2020 Emma Hardwick

ISBN: 9798631825215

Version: FTSG-0002-PK

BOOK CARD

Other books by Emma Hardwick

The Urchin of Walton Hall

The Sailor's Lost Daughters

The Scullery Maid's Salvation

The Widow of the Valley

The Christmas Songbird

The Slum Lady

The Vicar's Wife

The Lost Girl's Beacon of Hope

The Slum Sisters' Wish

Finley's Christmas Secret

The Lighthouse Keepers Lass

CONTENTS

Fleeing the Emerald Isle	9
The long walk to the quay	18
All aboard the coffin ship	23
Alone in London	28
Motionless through Wapping	32
Fetch Albin & Sons	40
This is 'Shilling' Everyone	48
The unusual change to the unusual routine	52
The exquisite Catherine Franco	58
But you don't drink, Samuel	65
Moving to the country and back again	70
Clean towels and clean sheets	74
The request for a peculiar gift	78
Meeting John Green in London	87
Taming Miss Wallace	99
The journey to France	107
The search for a second tutor	119
So, where did I come from, Papa?	124
The return to Wapping	128
Thank God that is over	138
Trusting one's gut instincts	146
Who did I see this morning	158
The announcement over dinner	164

The emerald necklace   168

A different sort of education   170

The return to Dorset   177

The move to booming Birmingham   191

There will be some changes, Mr Atherton   197

Shilling's formal address   204

The broken, beaten and the damned   213

The dark clouds of Buckingham strike again   218

Reviewing the day over dinner   226

THe news from the grapevine   231

The sound of broken glass   234

Visible and invisible wounds   242

The questionable appointment   250

Meet me at the botanical gardens   254

Looking for backing   259

The blood-splattered shirt   274

helping those less fortunate   278

The industrialists' gala dinner   289

The frantic wait   296

1

FLEEING THE EMERALD ISLE

Clare Byrne had been in labour for twelve hours when she arrived at the London dockside. It was an icy cold day in December, 1849, but she couldn't remember the exact date. She had spent four queasy days on the boat from Dublin to London. It was overcrowded, and the seas were rough. The hungry Irish were seasick, and their stomachs were empty. Their bodies heaved with nothing to give.

Clare didn't sleep much as the ship battled the rough waves whipped up by the English Channel. She was terrified on the journey but more terrified of going back to Ireland.

The London dockside was congested with people, carts and horses. The sky was dark. There was no promise that the bleak weather would lift as the fog and smoke choked the skies, making the air heavier than was natural.

She felt another contraction convulse through her—they were becoming more frequent and intense. It felt as though her intestines wanted to fall from her body. Her waters broke as she walked down the gangway, leaving her underwear sodden. There was no one to ask for help, and she began to panic. It was her first child, and Clare was frantic.

She was disoriented, the world was spinning about her, and the pain was all-engulfing. Every few minutes, she would stop to lean against something or hold onto a rail to steady her cramped body. Clare felt herself losing a grip on reality. *How much longer can I endure this?*

A few times, her vision began to tunnel, light fading to black and perspiration running down her back. Feeling she was on the cusp of fainting, she wanted to let everything go, to give up. She wanted the peace of oblivion.

People were shoving against Clare, shouting for her to move along; except she couldn't let go of the rail. A hail of insults and abuse rained down upon her. The small travelling bag she clutched was becoming difficult to carry. Soon, she felt unable to walk.

She could feel the pressure of the baby's head, slung low inside her. Desperate to lie down, there was only the gutter to sit in. It ran with raw sewage. She made it a few more paces to a clearer patch of ground. The severe chill was blowing through her tattered dress, and her soaking underwear was freezing and sticking to her legs, chafing them.

The agonising pain only had one benefit. It stopped her thinking of Finn laying on his mother's kitchen table, emaciated and dead. He was dressed in his wedding suit. It had fit so well on the day they married but now covered him like a shawl flowing over his body and draping loosely over his thin flesh.

The day Finn was buried, Clare focused her thoughts on the handsome man that she married on their gloriously happy wedding day, trying to extinguish thoughts of the last few dire months and the inevitable slide towards death. Willing her mind from the terrible present and into the delightful past, she watched him working in the field, focusing on his rough, calloused labourer's hands that had loved her so tenderly. *Oh, and that broad smile of a likeable rogue.* He had a loud sincere laugh that made his eyes wrinkle until you could hardly see them.

Every night she sheltered in his arms, and he would tell her:

> "I loved you from the first moment I saw you, and I will never let you go."

Back then, Clare could never imagine herself without him and would reply:

> "I want to love you forever, Finn Byrne, and one lifetime is not enough."

It gave him a lump in his throat. He felt the same way.

Before the Great Irish Hunger, Finn and Clare were tenant farmers on a large western Irish estate. The rental of the one-roomed cottage was so high that the income barely covered it, and left very little money for anything else.

Finn found a job on the Ashbury estate, and Clare tended the small piece of land that they lived on. Life wasn't easy, but it was happy. Days were hard work, but nights were absolutely pleasure-filled.

They were delighted with their small home. Clare kept it immaculate, and there was always a jug of wildflowers on the table to add a touch of delicate colour to the small room. To brighten up the place she had rescued a piece of lace from a discarded petticoat and hung it inside the only downstairs window of the cottage, which was actually a hole in the wall that allowed in light. Finn had done what he could to close it up. He made a 'pane' out of glass bottles of different colours that he framed with wood.

They had whitewashed the inside of the cottage. At night the orange flames reflected on the white walls, which made the room cosy and warm. The brightly coloured window could be seen by their neighbours across the valley.

The price for beef that season was exceptionally high. Lord Ashbury, the English landowner, was having a very profitable year, although nobody had ever seen the man. He could have been a ghost for all the locals knew. His son visited occasionally, but only to ensure that the manager wasn't stealing and that the tenants weren't being paid too much.

The staff at the big house provided meals for their master, enough food to feed a small country, then went off to their homes for a yet another bland, tiny dinner of potatoes and peas. Despite the significant commitment his staff showed, the profits of the estate never drifted down to the workers.

The potato crop failed in 1845, and the tenants had a tough time feeding their families. It was easier for Finn and Clare—they were only two, but their friends and neighbours had bigger families, and the struggle for food was much more acute for them.

The blight became progressively worse, with more significant percentages of the crops ruined. Finn lived in eternal hope that the next harvest would be better, but eventually, after a four-year struggle, the optimism faded as they accepted it would only be a matter of months before they were evicted from the tiny piece of land they were renting. *We're no more use to his lordship. It will be far more profitable to put cattle onto the small plot than people.*

Sir Ashbury showed no empathy for his tenants. Like so many privileged people, he never suffered any hardship and made sure he never witnessed it either. Neither could his privileged Lordship identify any individuals scraping a meagre existence on his land. Like many English settlers, he viewed the Irish as a defiant mass of Roman Catholics united in their hatred of Britain. They were loathsome, evil, dangerous and rebellious. *Cromwell had the right idea coming over to crush them and put them in their place.*

His Lordship, in his tyrannical mind, was never wrong. With privilege came great responsibility, and with the Great Lord watching over him giving his blessing, he watched the subjects on his land die of starvation. Those that didn't die were punished for any desperate act undertaken to feed their distraught families. Men now risked punishment for food. Anything from picking an apple, stealing a piglet to trapping a deer was theft and men were gaoled, transported or hanged for the most trifling of offences. Socially, the country was in chaos. If the masses had had the energy, there would have been war.

Financial woes forced Finn and his young wife to move into his mother's two-roomed cottage, which was more like a hovel than a home. Finn didn't know how long they would remain in that basic, draughty little dwelling, but he hoped that the landlord could be more lenient. For many years, his 'ma' had worked in the great house, and they all hoped there would be some recognition for that loyalty.

When they arrived at Mrs Byrne's doorstep, Clare was pregnant with their first child, and he was worried about her. The burden of finding food became greater and greater, and three people under one roof was proving to be a challenge. Friends and neighbours had long since left, and the countryside was becoming deserted. The small cadre of neighbours that were left helped each other as far as possible, but with the mass exodus, resources began to wane.

Hope walked alongside Finn, and so he never believed that he too would reach rock bottom. However, by the time he realised, in the winter of 1849, it was too late for him to leave. He was too sickly to make the hazardous journey. Besides, he only had the money for one fare to England. *Clare will have to go.* He promised he would follow, but knew on making the promise that he wouldn't make it.

It had been years now with no signs of the situation changing. Finn would share his meal with Clare at night, saying that someone he'd seen on the road had shared some bread with him earlier. He fed her with food and hope and himself with lies. It helped numb the fact he knew he was dying and he would never see his child grow or have Clare, the love of his life, in his arms till he was old.

A cautious man, Finn saved many tiny amounts of money over the year and kept it hidden for an emergency. It was worthless to buy food with—there was none. On the infrequent occasions, they did find something, it would be ridiculously overpriced. *No, this 'spare' money will buy Clare a passage to England—before she has the child.*

The government, led by British Prime Minister Lord Russell, tried to usher in new laws to assist the starving masses. However, it was too little too late. Worse, the wealthy landowners voted against most of the plans for relief. The English plantation owners always won. Some had never seen the estates they inherited let alone the staff that managed them.

In his final weeks, Finn knew he didn't have long to live. On one of the last bittersweet evenings with his wife, he took the savings from under the floorboards and made Clare promise that she would find a passage to England if he died. She made the oath, but she was beside herself with the early onset of grief. *Why is there nothing I can do to keep him alive? I can't imagine sitting here watching him die, but that is what I must do.*

Seeing her deep in thought, he squeezed her hand to get her attention.

> "Perhaps," said Finn "you can find Sophie, Jack Connolly's daughter. She is in London. Go to her mother in Dublin and get her address, then take a boat to England and find her."

The man, once vibrant and energetic was now a bony, barely breathing skeleton of a human. Clare could do nothing; she was close to the end herself. She knew that she was only alive because Finn fed her his quota of 'nourishment'.

Thank God Finn drifted to death in his sleep, that is 'something'. The trip to Dublin would be exhausting, as she joined the throngs of starving people in their trek eastward, hoping for food or emigration or both.

2

THE LONG WALK TO THE QUAY

As she walked, she grieved. The anguish she felt became misery. The child in her tummy was her only motivation to go to England. If she were not pregnant, she would have laid on the side of the road and died right there.

By now, almost a million people had perished, and another million had emigrated from Ireland as refugees. Along the 'Road of Horror,' as Clare began to call it, she witnessed children moaning, far beyond any help. Mothers wailed with limp infants dying in their arms. Thousands of starving walkers wasted away, dying where they collapsed.

The men are the most tragic. They are defeated and emasculated watching their families suffering, and there is nothing they can do about it. How can this be allowed to happen?

Ireland was making an excellent job of exporting other food to England. Large ships left every day, laden with tonnes of cattle, beef, mutton, peas, butter and honey. Nobody could convince Clare that this was about potatoes. This was murder. Nothing had changed for the rich. *They would feed their dog a whole chicken before they gave a hungry man a slice of bread.* It was barbaric and dehumanising. Sometimes, the selfish betrayal felt worse than the situation.

Clare was filled with shame as she walked into the city.

A fellow walker picked up on her sorrow.

> "Cheer up, lassie. Don't be so hard on yourself. There's so many of us raggedy folk here, you're invisible."

As the long train of rags passed through Dublin, people gathered along the pavements and watched as if they saw freaks in a travelling show. But instead of the crowd being loud and jovial, the silence was deafening. No one came forward to help. It was as though the situation was so hopeless, nothing would solve it, so nobody tried.

Her walking companion was right, she was anonymous in the crowd, and it was a liberating if lonely thought. From other talks she heard on the road, she concluded that if God did not exact justice on the British, the Irish would. Clare's body was exhausted, but her soul was on fire for righteousness. Powerfully, the child in her belly kicked in agreement.

Arriving in Dublin posed its own problems. An unfamiliar Clare now had to find her way to Sophie's mother's house. But the Irish luck was with Clare on that day. A young man took pity on her as she collapsed to the curb, close to a pub. He didn't look too healthy himself, but he poured her half his beer and gave her a slice of bread and butter. For years, she had not eaten a meal as tasty as this one. It was the kindness, not the meal, that overwhelmed her.

Clare thanked the young man with all her heart and then wept. The stranger tenderly embraced her hand. It was the first warm, genuine human contact she had experienced since she began the long walk. After explaining that she was looking for someone, the kind young man memorised the address and went to find Anna Connolly.

The youth remembered to mention that Clare was pregnant, so Mrs Connolly arrived with a small cart and donkey. She had anticipated that Clare would be in no condition to walk the final half-mile to her house. Anna Connolly was filled with energy. She and the young man, now introduced as Luke, lifted Clare onto the back of the cart. It was lined with hay to ease the journey.

After a short while, they reached Anna's home. It was a tiny townhouse with a kitchen and parlour downstairs and two rooms upstairs, but to Clare, it was a palace. Anna had a meagre income from her late husband's estate that just kept a roof over her head, with enough spare for a few treats. The house was small, clean and warm.

St Patrick's Catholic Church in the local parish had started a support group and sponsored church members to feed the refugees. Anna subscribed to the charity, never forgetting her humble roots.

The poor expectant mother hadn't eaten properly for a long time, so Anna gave her a nutritious but light vegetable and bone broth that was easy to digest. Clare was amazed at how little she could eat before feeling very full. The food and warmth were soothing, and Clare fell asleep beside the small kitchen table.

She awoke on the settee in the parlour with a blanket covering her—she had slept for sixteen hours. The fire burnt in the grate, and there was a delicious smell coming from the kitchen. Anna fed her more broth and cups of tea, to which a small sugar cube was added.

Anna organised some hot water, and Clare washed. She rinsed the black filth from her hair, and when she was done, Anna saw a dark-haired, green-eyed angel in front of her. Anna explained that she could stay for three nights until her ship left port, but would have to share a bed with her. The other bedrooms were taken up by families who were leaving for America.

For Clare, this was more grace and kindness than she'd ever anticipated. On the last morning of her stay, Anna packed food for her trip to London, tied it in oilcloth and gave Clare Sophie's address in London. Having experienced several acts of human kindness in a very short time, Clare Byrne allowed herself to hope.

3

ALL ABOARD THE
COFFIN SHIP

The day of the sailing came, and the quays were busy with the clatter of horses' hooves, the rumble of cart and barrow wheels and the shout of dockers unloading the cargo.

Clutching her precious ticket, an anxious Clare joined a long line of famine victims awaiting to embark. It was a troubled time. A few weeks earlier, a ship bound for Canada had sunk, driven by a storm onto the sharp rocky coastline, only a few miles from Dublin, with all souls aboard lost. Despite the horror stories, the exodus continued unabated. The queue Clare joined still stretched over a mile from the docks.

Fortunately, Anna had purchased Clare's genuine steerage ticket. The unscrupulous often forged the permits and sold them to those who were too weak to care, or too exhausted to know that they would be denied their passage.

There was little time for tears or farewells, as Claire, along with her fellow travellers, were herded onto the ship like cattle. Besides, Anna had to get back to help more of the famished. The flow of people still desperately in need of salvation showed no sign of slowing.

The frantic attempts by the impoverished to sneak on board meant stowing away was common. Some dived in the water and hoped to board the ship, through means fair or foul. Small children were hidden in luggage.

Clare learned that as part of the preparations to sail, there was a roll call. Seven people were frogmarched off the ship before it finally left port. *How did they even board it? The checks were rigorous?* In the confusion, Clare heard someone complain their bag had been stolen already. She clung to hers even more tightly.

In steerage class, on a woefully overcrowded ship, she was to be crammed below decks. Most of the bunks were taken out so more people could be stuffed in. The complement of people on board was hundreds above the official capacity with the insurers. If she were to get a bunk to rest in, Clare hoped it would be the uppermost one. Being below a seasick fellow traveller did not bear thinking about. Tired and not really sure what to do, she slid her back down against the edge of the hull and sat leaning against it. On deck next to her, a family of nine were struggling to organise themselves in little more space.

The conditions were awful below deck. The floors of the living areas were supposed to be cleaned by the crew, but they never were. The sanitary conditions were in a terrible state. Disease and starvation picked off the weakest—the young and the old—from the first day afloat.

The threat of fever was never far away with everyone squashed like sardines into the cramped space below deck. Once someone succumbed to it, it would spread like wildfire. Being shut up in the dark with fever victims made some passengers panic. The moaning and groaning of the sick and the dying were enough to keep them awake all night. Once they were far enough away from the shore, the corpses were dragged up on deck, wrapped in sailcloth and dumped overboard. This gruesome activity happened several times a day.

Hoping they were finally off to a better life in England, a few people sang a few ditties and clapped along to pass the time. After an hour, they were too weak to continue and had to give up.

Cooking was done on deck, using fireboxes. These were stout wooden crates filled with hot bricks. Clare was lucky enough to share with the family of nine who had taken pity on the young widow. It saved her battling with the little pan Anna gave her. The big pot was easier to stir and the contents less likely to burn.

The food was meagre, and only a quarter the amount that was promised beforehand to paying passengers. Basics like stale bread, mouldy biscuits, or powdered goods like flour, rice and oatmeal were all that was on offer.

Water was rationed, with a generous five gallons—not that you would want to drink it. It was foetid, stored in wooden barrels, thoroughly unsuited to the task.

As a woman, there would be no chance for Claire to work as a crew member to try and get more food. Many passengers questioned if it was worth it anyway. Those men that wasted what remained of their sapped strength to assist were often beaten for making a mistake, and their extra rations were never forthcoming.

At the end of mealtimes, a young lad came by and sloshed water into the boxes. Asking why he was doing that given the difficulty to heat them, those onboard were horrified to discover a recent fire happened on a vessel leaving the Port of Liverpool, with seventy souls perishing. With very few lifeboats, a blaze on board would have been catastrophic. Everyone then checked the fireboxes were put out.

During stormy crossings, anything that wasn't tied down got tossed about from one side of the ship to the other, whether that was people or boxes or barrels, or even the dead. Everything would land in one big heap. Clare avoided seeking shelter in any small rooms below deck. With another grim proclamation, she had learned sixty-eight people on another ship had perished. Their mistake was trying to protect themselves from the flying debris, hiding in a small storeroom. They were so badly crushed they could no longer breathe, or escape. Suffocation, it was hoped, was swift. Considering the alternative, being bombarded with flying objects seemed a little more bearable.

The ship was in an awful condition, barely seaworthy. As it sailed through a storm, there was a sense of dread that the hull might break.

Depending on the direction it was tacking, the ship's uncaulked interior wood would flex, and gaps would open inside the vessel. It had a knack of trapping women's skirts, or inquisitive children's tiny fingers. They would not be released until the ship changed tack again, often several hours later.

With little idea where they were, once the rocky Irish coastline was out of view, all they could do was look for smaller boats or a flock of sea birds to provide a clue they were closer to their final destination.

Time passed very slowly, indeed.

3

ALONE IN LONDON

At the docks, there were runners, lithe young men sporting bright green waistcoats designed to attract the newly landed Irish. Anna said they were to be avoided, keen to steal the luggage and fence the contents or hide it to extort exorbitant fees for its return.

The underhanded dealings meant scuffles often broke out, with some unwary travellers who dared to complain punched in the face and left with a broken jaw to add to their troubles.

By now, every step Clare made had to be a conscious decision. She forced herself to walk down the gangway and through the mass of people, then headed towards a quieter side street. Sophie's address was in her pocket, but she had no energy to take it out.

Not making it to the side street, she leaned against a red-brick wall by the quayside. The pain, fear and hopelessness overtook her. She cast aside her pride and approached a man walking towards her. She made eye contact and took a few steps in his direction. He began to walk faster to avoid her. She approached a young woman.

"Please," she begged, "please help me."

The closest the woman could come to showing kindness was to point her down the road towards the nearest mission that helped disadvantaged women.

Now, she could hardly breathe and the last person she remembered speaking to said something about 'bloody Irish leeches'.

She used the last of her strength to stumble somewhere quieter. Once there, Clare could no longer stand. She collapsed onto her haunches, the full pressure of her upper body onto her stomach forced the baby further down the birth canal. She felt her flesh rip apart and something slither from her body.

The pain subsided, she toppled over onto her side. Her body naturally expelled the placenta without her knowledge. She had no last thoughts about the baby as the light began to recede. She only clung to her fond memories of Finn, and she was overwhelmed by a painless peace. The light faded. Clare was dead.

Margaret Carrott watched the whole event from the steps where she stood. It was always an excellent spot to see what was happening. She had a tired face. It didn't have the energy to smile, and if it could, there would only be a few teeth on show. All the lines of her face ran vertically, and with her sagging jowls, her face looked more like a sad old bloodhound.

Margaret was permanently protected by a considerable army overcoat. It fitted her more like a tent. 'Maggie' as they called her, could stash all her worldly belongings inside that coat. Like a tortoise, she took her home with her. Her auburn-grey lice-infested hair was shoved into a floppy red felt hat, its wide brim dropping below her eyes, creating a witchy and eerie appearance.

Maggie moved toward Clare and nudged her with her foot. The thin corpse flopped from its side onto its back, with the skirt up about its waist. The underwear was blood-soaked, but there was a mewing sound, quiet as a whisper. The soaked drawers moved slightly.

"Oh, mother of God!" whispered Maggie to
herself. "'ere's a baby. A wee baby, I tell yer!"

By now there was a small crowd forming around the poor dead girl on the floor. Maggie yanked down the soiled drawers and grabbed the child with the placenta trailing behind it. One of the dockers with a knife severed the cord and tied a knot.

By now, the child was screaming from cold and the instinct to feed. The crowd was debating what to do with the infant, Maggie grabbed the child away from the man and stuffed it under her greatcoat. In the warmth and the darkness, the confused baby relaxed and then fell silent.

However, nothing was to be nurturing or noble about Maggie's intentions that day.

5

MOTIONLESS THROUGH WAPPING

Samuel Hudson's carriage turned into the street at a sedate pace. If it had been going any faster, the horses would have ploughed into the crowd that stood around Clare's body blocking the street. The excitement drew mostly vagrants as the road bordered a slum. By now about sixty people were gathered around the body with more arriving by the minute. It would not be long before journalists began to appear. The public was obsessed with any sort of violence—it sold a lot of newspapers.

Many of the observers were children who became excited when they saw anything gory. Later on, they could explain every tiny detail to their family, friends and neighbours. Each time the story was retold, a little more artistic license would be used, a little zest added, which would gain them even more attention.

There was considerable speculation about what had happened to the girl. Theories were abundant. Was she murdered? Had she been ill? Was there really a baby? If so, was it alive, or dead? The crowd was so captivated by the action ahead that few even noticed the stranded cab and horses behind them.

Samuel's employee, Socrates, who had been working for him for some years, slowed his master's cab to a halt and lithely jumped down from his seat. There was no chance of turning the horses around in the narrow, cobbled street. The only option was to go forward. Keen to see what was causing the obstruction, he began to weave his way to the edge of the crowd. *The cause of the bottleneck has to be quite impressive to draw this size of impromptu gathering.*

"What's holding up the traffic?" asked Socrates.

"Someone has died down there in the street. That's what they say." mumbled a man next to him.

This was not unusual for the slums of London. Crime prospered in the most impoverished areas, and desperate people had to be creative to keep their families fed. More often than not, it was just good old-fashioned law-breaking. Perhaps someone lightly coshed over the head for some meagre pickings from their pockets. This time, the unlucky quarry would not be staggering away with a headache.

Whatever lurks there must be quite a sight to keep this hardened crowd engrossed for such a long time. Socrates made an attempt to push himself through the throng. *Oh, blast! Where are the bobbies when you need them? They'd shift this lot in a flash.*

The crowd didn't give an inch, and Socrates found himself beginning to be swallowed up by the mob behind him as more people crammed to join the throng. He stood on his tiptoes to try and glimpse just beyond the people at the centre of the drama. He could only catch sight of something reddish, perhaps a woman's floppy hat, but other than that, nothing.

Deciding he needed to be more resourceful to find the answer, he noticed a flight of stairs leading up the side of a building. Making his way over to them, he was disappointed to find they too were also filling up with observers. Thankfully, able to barge his way up to the second step, he managed to see it was indeed a woman wearing a red felt hat with some orangey-grey hair sticking out here and there. She was in the centre of the throng, the focus of it. The crowd seemed to be yelling at her angrily. She clutched her coat close to her body as if she was cold.

By this time, Samuel Hudson had become increasingly frustrated, sitting in the motionless cab. His fob watch showed that he had been waiting for nigh on twenty minutes. His patience was wearing thin. Indeed, he had spent a maddening afternoon discussing a social improvement plan for the underprivileged.

The government's Committee for Social Development in London typified a complex, slow and sluggish bureaucracy with no insight or creativity. For every solution he proposed, the committee devised at least one problem, and after a three-hour impasse this afternoon, he was tempted to abandon the project. Only his conscience kept him there. The personal relief from turning his back on the committee would have served no purpose for the large number of poor unfortunates depending upon him to represent them.

Samuel got out of the cab and scanned the area, looking for Socrates. *Where the hell are you, man?* He hung back from the crowd, not wanting to be engulfed by them. Noticing the group viewing the episode from the staircase, he glanced up and saw Socrates, now on one of the landings. He was straining his neck to get a better view of the action. Samuel gave his usual loud whistle, and everyone turned and stared at him, but it had the desired effect. Socrates whistled back, waved to his boss and scurried down the stairs.

"What's all the kerfuffle about over there?" asked Samuel, the irritation showing in his voice.

"Sir," answered Socrates, "there is a strange, crazed lady causing it. Everyone seems to be yelling at her. She is yelling back. Someone else mentioned a body, but I have not seen it with my own eyes. More than that, I have no clue."

Socrates sighed as Samuel's frustration flooded his expression. *As if today wasn't bad enough, now there's the master's temper to contend with.*

"Sir, I am sure that if we move the horses forward very slowly the crowd will make way for them and we will see what's happening up front."

Samuel nodded his head and climbed back into the cab. Socrates hopped onto the driver's seat and tentatively proceeded to nudge the horses forward. It was a tricky operation. *If the horses are startled by the crowd and bolt, they will trample the people. I need to avoid that at all costs. Easy does it now.* The coach began to move forward, albeit at a snail's pace. The crowd recognised the coach must belong to 'a dignitary' and with resentment dispersed to give it room to pass.

Eventually, they reached the front of the crowd, eager to be nearly clear of the drama and finally homeward bound. However, they were prevented from going any further because in front of the cab stood the wretched woman in the hat and trench coat. She was still involved in a heated argument with the bystanders beyond the coach.

"Getaway, getaway, mother of God, can't you leave an old woman alone? No, I'm not going to take off the coat, I don't know where the bairn went. Get! Get!"

The crowd was irate. People were hurling abuse at the old woman.

"I don't know who the girl is she yelled, I just got here, and probably somebody clobbered her over the head."

"We saw you take the bairn, Maggie. She's a wee baby, she'll die."

"Leave me be! I ain't got nuffin'. Someone else took it." yelled Maggie, keeping both hands on the coat.

Samuel, in a fit of annoyance, climbed out of the coach. The crowd became quiet at the site of the gentleman. He displayed signs of authority, and they seemed to expect him to provide a solution to the problem they were witnessing. There was a man at the front of the crowd yelling the loudest abuse at Margaret Carrott. Samuel walked up to him and asked him to step aside for a moment.

"What is happening with this woman? Why are you arguing?" Samuel asked without introducing himself.

"Well, Guv, we fink that Maggie there got a baby off that there dead lass and it's 'idden in her coat. She says she ain't gorrit, but we don't believe 'er.

Maggie, she be known for lifting kids, especially dead 'uns. See, she sells 'em to the men who cuts 'em up at the 'ospital. She's got a good little thing goin' there, Guv. She collects the bairns from the whores, and then she sells 'em. She ain't poor—she just looks poor. She's evil. She only wears that coat to 'ide the bairns. We cannae catch her, Guv, but maybe today's the day. God help us all."

Though the man lacked an education and the correct terminology, Samuel was able to understand what he was accusing her of.

Samuel was about to approach Margaret Carrott but stopped. He had glimpsed the terrible sight of some of Clare Byrne's corpse, lying on the floor, a short distance behind Maggie. He moved around the old crone very slowly and walked towards the body to get a better view. He stopped a little way from it, and then stood very still. Samuel had witnessed a lot in life, but he was not prepared for what he saw before him.

Laid on her back, with her head rolled fully to one side, was a striking young woman. Her ebony-coloured hair partially covered the beautiful translucent skin on her cheek—skin that looked cold and perfect. The other cheek lay against the filthy cobbles and had tiny specks of gravel embedded in the flesh from the impact of falling. The face was peaceful. *Oh, what a beautiful angel! And how sad it is that such a young life could be cut so brutally short.*

His eyes moved from her face and down towards her slender body. Her ragged skirt was still hitched around her waist. He saw the bloody underwear that was lying beside her. Her legs were splayed awkwardly, and the bottom half of her body was lying in a pool of maroon, congealed blood.

He wanted to weep but had to appear strong. *Oh, Lord above! Why are you doing this to me?* He was close to losing control.

6

FETCH ALBIN & SONS

A hush fell over the crowd, all eyes were on the gentleman, still wondering what he would do to resolve the crisis. Samuel stared at Clare for what seemed like hours to him, but really was only a few seconds. His mind absorbed every gory detail like a reluctant sponge. He suddenly felt freezing cold, and the frustration of his slow journey home had been replaced with a grim sense of emptiness inside.

The iron-grey sky above them was oppressive, and he wanted to run but couldn't. It was his duty to stay. He tried very hard to create order in his chaotic mind. He could not grasp a single thought that could help stabilise his emotions. He had felt this way before, paralysed. He was beside himself with grief. All he wanted to do was run far away and never look back.

A quiet voice next to him said:

"Sir?"

A hand touched his elbow but didn't attempt to manoeuvre him away from the sight. Socrates would protect Samuel's dignity, always allowing him to move in his own time, at his own pace.

"Sir?" he reassured again quietly.

As Samuel turned around to acknowledge Socrates, he heard a sound—a piercing sound. It was an outraged cry, and it was very close to them.

Instantly, Samuel's mind gained clarity. He spun on his heels and came face to face with Maggie Carrott.

"Give it to me!" he commanded.

"It is my wee little niece, Mister, I'm on my way to 'er mother's place. I look after the bairn while 'er mother works. I only nipped out for a moment."

Maggie gave him her most charming toothless smile. It didn't work on him. The crowd began to stir again. Voices began shouting:

"Give 'im the bairn, yer mad dog."

The situation was becoming dangerous and could worsen rapidly, turning into a riot.

Samuel moved closer to Maggie Carrott. Only Socrates and he heard the words spoken. They were whispered but had the effect of thunder. Maggie took two steps back, and her blood chilled. Socrates would hear Samuel repeat the same words many years later:

"If you harm my child, I will kill you!"

How Samuel developed the bond with the child so quickly was a mystery, but at that moment, he simply knew he would take the infant home. *There will be no debate about this. The matter is settled.*

Maggie had to maintain some sort of pride in front of the crowd, and she screamed hysterically:

"You can buy 'er if yer wants 'er so bad then—"

Maggie opened her coat which revealed the smallest little baby Samuel had ever seen. She removed the screaming child from a large interior pocket with one hand and cruelly dangled it by the arm in front of him.

"—How much, Madam?" interrupted Socrates.

He was confident that Samuel would strangle the woman if he got any closer, and he thought it best to move in between the two warring factions.

"One shilling," screamed Maggie Carrott. "I'll give yer the bairn for one shilling."

Samuel reached into his pocket and removed a small silver coin. He passed it to Socrates.

"Give her the money. I never want to see this heartless witch again."

With that, Samuel waited for Socrates to pass him the new-born, then turned and walked to the cab and climbed inside. He wrapped the baby in a blanket that he used when it was cold. He parted the cloth to look at the little face. She was small, furious, starving and unhappy. He hoped the lengthening pauses between the screaming bouts showed the little creature seemed to be calmed by her new owner and not that hunger was weakening her too.

From the cab, Samuel instructed a flustered Socrates to arrange a decent burial for Clare Byrne, which reminded his employee he knew nothing about raising babies, had little experience with undertakers, but was nevertheless, a resourceful assistant.

Socrates's first step was to pay someone to watch the body until he could arrange an undertaker to collect it. He looked about and saw a young man in his early twenties leaning against a wall, observing the situation. He looked clean and was well dressed for that area. Socrates hopped off the cab and approached the man. He introduced himself and asked if the fellow saw fit to look after the body until the undertaker arrived. They negotiated a price, and the young man accepted the offer.

Then, he employed another slightly older chap to fetch the undertaker, Albin & Sons, two streets down. They would send a wicker basket to collect the girl. Socrates gave the man Samuel's calling card and told him to pass the message to the undertaker to confirm that someone would be back to pay the bill.

Socrates steered the cab down the small side street. Next, he knew that he would have to find a wet nurse to feed the baby. *But where would I find one?* Across the road, he saw a charitable office that helped widows. Socrates dodged the horses and carts and reached the door in a short sprint. The women who worked at the charity were made of stern stuff and stared at him as he burst through the door.

Socrates introduced himself to Mrs Wright, who was sat beside a sturdy-looking desk. She was polite and efficient while assisting him.

She knew of a young woman of clean and sober habits, a widow who had lost a child in the last few days and suggested perhaps Socrates could approach her. He agreed.

Socrates and Samuel took the coach to the address. The lady who lived there, Annabelle, opened the door to her humble abode. It was a single room in a depressing tenement building. She barely had enough money for it, and soon, she would be relying on a doss house coffin bed, crammed in a tiny room with forty, or more, other souls. As a widow, she would need to find a husband very quickly to make ends meet.

She looked at the visitor with a soulless expression. Socrates approached her kindly, sensing her sorrow. She was so emotional that she struggled to talk and after a few attempts decided to keep quiet until she was asked a question. Showing his routine respect and compassion, Socrates politely asked for her name.

"Annabelle Lambeth," came the softly spoken reply.

Socrates explained that his employer Mr Hudson required a wet nurse and that her name had been recommended by Mrs Wright.

Although her delicate features were heavenly, the light in her eyes had been extinguished with grief, and she had no desire to ever smile again. She seemed distant, despite putting in a lot of effort to listen. Socrates, however, needed a wet nurse now and, for him, it was time to be blunt.

> "The child is sobbing, slowly starving in that cab.
> Do you want the job?"

Knowing that this would be her most sensible option, for the time being at least, Annabelle answered 'yes' without emotion, packed her paltry possessions into a tattered sack and left the past behind. She didn't close the door. She didn't care. She never ever wanted to return to that room full of terrible memories.

With the assistance of Socrates Annabelle climbed into the cab.

"Good evening, Miss." Samuel greeted her courteously.

"Good evening," she replied. He didn't care if she omitted 'sir' from her response, he wasn't that sort of man.

"Do you have any experience wet nursing?"

"Just a day or two, with my own young 'un." she replied, looking dejected.

Seeing her crestfallen expression, Samuel's tone became even more sympathetic.

"Yes, Mrs Wright told us about your terrible situation. I am so sorry to hear of your hardship of late. But it does mean you can help us to feed this baby and keep her alive. We will take care of you in return. There is space in my home to secure you some lodgings. Would you be able to take care of her?"

"Aye, I came from a large family, and we all helped mother look after the little 'uns when she needed a rest," replied Annabel, not in a position to turn any offer of work down, regardless of how she might feel about it.

"So, it's settled, you will come home with us?" confirmed Samuel with a slight desperation in his deep voice.

"Yes."

"Thank you. Socrates will negotiate your wages. I trust that will be satisfactory. I am Samuel Hudson, Madam" he said to the anxious woman next to him, who wondered what the next chapter of her life had in store for her.

"And, Miss Annabelle, at this moment, you are the most important person in all our lives."

His gaze turned gently towards the little baby. The woman's nervousness lowered a fraction on hearing the compliment. Nobody of Samuel's class had ever spoken to her so kindly before today. For all her sorrow, she was taken aback by it. It was a little glimmer of warmth after all the hardship these past few days and was most welcome.

He passed the baby to her. She opened her blouse and exposed a breast unashamedly. To preserve her dignity, Samuel had lowered the blinds, and it was quite dark inside the cab. The baby smelled the milk, her mouth opened a little, and the tiny head moved from side to side; the reflex to feed emerged instinctively. Annabelle slipped the nipple into the baby's mouth. The infant latched on and began to suckle frantically. For the first time, the baby seemed genuinely content and restful. Samuel knew that, somehow, things were going to be just fine.

7

THIS IS 'SHILLING' EVERYONE

Socrates had left Samuel and Miss Annabelle in the cab, stating he would be back shortly. He walked the few streets to where Clare hopefully still lay. *Please don't let a rogue masquerading as a relative have donated her to an anatomy school.* Relieved, he saw the young man paid to stand on watch was still there, and he had shown the foresight to cover most of her with his coat, shielding her poor defenceless body from the gawps of the ragged, titillated onlookers.

Now that there was nothing explicit to see, the crowd had lost interest and slowly dispersed. Albin & Sons arrived a few minutes after Socrates. He was determined to ensure that the body was treated with respect. He took it upon himself to direct the process. It burdened the undertakers somewhat, and they were mildly annoyed by the interference, but Socrates was faithful to Samuel and would always ensure that his orders were followed to the letter.

The undertakers returned the coat to the owner and wrapped Clare in a sheet. They put the body into the basket coffin used to sheathe the dead from prying eyes and make the task at hand more manageable, then lifted her onto the cart with the utmost reverence. In her small bag, still, on her arm, they found her ticket with her name on it. They passed it onto Socrates, who took note of the details, then promptly paid the fees for her collection and burial.

Time had seemed to fly swiftly by since the cab had edged towards the horde of bystanders. The four weary travellers arrived at the Hudson Mayfair home long after dark. The lamps in the entrance hall were lit in anticipation of his arrival.

Socrates entered the house and began to rally the staff together with the gusto of a Sergeant Major. They presented themselves in the downstairs hallway to await the fiasco they believed was in store for them. Samuel only attended scheduled events as a general rule, and to arrive home unexpectedly this late usually meant something significant had happened.

Slowly, Samuel opened the cab door and jumped out. He pulled out the step for Annabelle, and she handed him the baby to hold while she climbed out. She took the baby out of his arms and held her. Samuel hadn't got to see the woman properly since the blinds had been drawn as she fed the infant.

As she walked into the light, Samuel stopped in his tracks. In front of him was a beautiful, svelte young woman, blonde hair, skin like ivory and enormous blue eyes.

For a short while, the staff couldn't believe what they were seeing. Here was their master, with a strange woman holding an undressed new-born inside a blanket.

> "We have a new addition to the family" yelled Socrates joyfully. "Well, what are you waiting for? Prepare a room for Miss Annabelle and the baby for the night. Get some hot tea and warm food on the go right this minute. Master Samuel is famished. Oh, and heat up some water to wash the baby in."

Socrates was so loud shouting orders it only added to their confusion. *Why is he treating this as business as usual, when the situation is most unusual indeed?* A little like Mr Hudson, the staff wore big, if mystified, smiles as they scurried off to do the tasks. The house was alive again.

Samuel insisted that Clare's remains be buried in his family plot at the cemetery in Highgate. Samuel felt he had to show Shilling's mother respect; she had provided him with a daughter after all.

A few days later, Samuel and Socrates went to the grave-yard for the internment. They had correctly guessed that Clare was Catholic from the ticket and they, together with an Irish Roman Catholic priest Father O'Connell who was to conduct the service, said farewell to Clare. No one else was present.

The moment they entered the cemetery, the clouds parted for the first time in days, and the sun shone through. They ambled reluctantly towards the burial plot. As the light touched the raindrops that littered the trees, grass and flowers, curiously the world began to sparkle, on such a sad day.

The coffin was slowly lowered into the earth while the priest spoke in hushed, respectful tones. At the last 'Amen', Samuel turned and walked away, leaving Socrates to extend the relevant courtesies to the priest. There had been too much death in his life of late, and he was keen to leave the graveside. He could barely look at the other names on the memorial.

Later that evening, Samuel went up to the nursery. Miss Annabelle was settling the baby into a wicker crib.

Samuel leaned over the edge and stared at the child.

I will name her Alexandra Hudson, but I will always call her 'Shilling'.

8

THE UNUSUAL CHANGE TO THE UNUSUAL ROUTINE

Samuel Hudson woke up every morning to a different day, and he would have it no other way. The idea of living the same predictable existence for the rest of his life was unacceptable.

Samuel marched to the beat of his own drum which antagonised the power-hungry elitists and aristocrats. He was that rare individual who could embrace success and maintain humility. He took command of his household without raising his voice and thought carefully before he spoke.

He was a social enigma who made well-to-do people uneasy with his lack of ceremony and loathing of protocol. He was oblivious to class, and he didn't foster the habit of judging people by the clothes they wore, the company they kept or cutlery they used.

Women preferred to avoid him because he refused to be moulded by societal norms, airs and graces. The church had given up on him long ago. He wouldn't wear a wig or dress like a dandy. His circle of contacts represented all cross-sections of society from gentry to fitters that worked at his Birmingham factories.

By choice, Samuel had few friends, but the people he invited into his life were kind and devoted to him. There was no haughtiness. Everyone simply called him 'Samuel' and not 'Sir', although Socrates still struggled with that.

Since the baby girl arrived merely a few weeks ago, Samuel Hudson had broken his own rule and developed two new rituals. The first was going to the nursery every morning at seven to visit little Shilling and have a cup of tea with 'Miss Annabelle'. The second, in the evening, he spent at least two hours in the nursery. He would sit in his regular chair, cradling her, thinking about the future—a future that was to be brighter—for both of them.

It was customary for Samuel to knock on the nursery door before he entered. It was a courtesy he showed to Miss Annabelle since she could be feeding the baby, and he did not want to embarrass her. In the beginning, she was taken aback by the regular visits. Most fathers would not see their children until they were five; usually, as they were putting them into a coach and sending them to a school far away. As always, Samuel Hudson was a conundrum.

Miss Annabelle opened the door and put her finger to her lips, asking him to be quiet. The curtains of the nursery were still closed, and the room was dark and warm. It was the start of spring, but it was still only just daybreak outside.

Samuel walked to the crib and gazed into it. Shilling was swaddled in a warm blanket. She wore a small pink nightcap and her little face, turned delicately to one side, was a vision of absolute tranquillity.

"So, Miss Annabelle, how did the princess sleep last night?" he enquired, bursting with fatherly pride.

"I only had to wake up once, Samuel. Quite soon she will be sleeping through the night."

It still feels strange calling him Samuel, but he will insist.

There was a gentle knock on the half-open door and Lizzy, one of the housemaids, entered holding a tea tray. Annabelle took it from her and put it onto a small table placed between two comfortable chairs. That morning, she and Samuel would chat for an hour. In the beginning, they only spoke about the practicalities of raising Shilling, but these days they talked about more.

For once, Samuel was quiet for a while, staring thoughtfully at the steam rising out of his cup.

"Miss Annabelle," he said softly, "I would like to ask you something, if I may? Feel free to say it's not my business, but I have had this on my mind for a long time."

Annabelle peered over her cup. She wondered if it was a romantic question and hoped it wasn't.

"I know that your child passed away, but I know nothing else about you as a person. You have never had a day off. You never speak about your family. You mentioned in the cab on the night I first met you that you had experience looking after your younger siblings, and yet you never mention any of them. I am curious and, I must confess, a little worried about you."

"I have nothing to go back to, Samuel—" she trailed off, clearly keen to close down the discussion.

They sat in silence for a while. Samuel was tongue-tied as his mind raced. There were things he felt he wanted to tell her, but he got no pleasure delving into his past. Neither, it seemed, did she. Thankfully, the delicate subject was quickly forgotten as Shilling began to stir.

Later that morning, Samuel called Socrates into his study.

"I want you to take care of Miss Annabelle, please. Make sure she wants for nothing."

"Yes, Sir."

"Socrates, I don't know the whole story, but she has suffered like no one should. We know that she lost her child within a matter of days, and I fear the cruel reaper has taken more of her family, possibly in rapid succession. I, of all people, know what that feels like. I don't want her left abandoned when Shilling no longer needs wet nursing. She has been through too much to be alone. Let's make her feel welcome but please avoid looking too far into the future—I fear she would be daunted by the thought of it. We need to make provision for her during Shilling's early years. She is her saviour and should be rewarded for that."

Now under strict orders to see to Annabelle's wellbeing, Socrates instructed the kitchen to take her regular meals. Lizzy was appointed to watch the child for two hours in the late afternoon, so Annabelle could have a much-needed rest. It was also the time the young wet nurse dined with the other staff and had time to attend to her own affairs, before returning to the nursery to attend to Shilling.

Socrates also insisted that the staff go by the nursery regularly and talk to her, so she did not feel isolated in the big house.

One of the best parts of the morning for Annabelle was when cook had a brief break for elevenses and would pop up with tea and treats. They would spend a short while talking. Even now, Annabelle would sometimes smile but never laugh.

On one such morning meeting, Annabelle mentioned to cook that Samuel ran his home very differently to other wealthy people. Cook looked at her, kindly.

"Mr Samuel is a good man Annabelle, he has his demons, but he never shares them with anybody."

9

THE EXQUISITE CATHERINE FRANCO

Samuel's business was expanding rapidly. He recently received an order to manufacture even more train wheels. The railway systems were growing at a rapid pace, in England with eight thousand miles of track recently ordered by the government. New lines were also extending to the colonies, India, Jamaica, British Guyana and more.

Though he trusted his managers to oversee operations in the Midlands, Samuel was too much of a perfectionist to allow them to run his factory independently. He always had a hand on the tiller. He had built his business from the ground up, starting in the steel industry. Although he was raised on a farm, at a young age, he developed an interest in steam power and the efficiencies it brought. He had heard what it had done for the cotton mills. He rented space in a small blacksmith's foundry. There he began casting much-improved agricultural implements to assist with the new steam-powered farming practices. He began working by hand and then became more mechanised as demand grew. Soon, he could invest in the business. By twenty-six, Samuel Hudson was a millionaire.

It was not an easy path to follow, and he took many risks when he first started in the business world. His first decision was to never employ children. There were plenty of unemployed men who needed a decent wage to support their families. He had the theory that even though child labour was cheap, they were less efficient. Besides, his business didn't require them to crawl into small spaces,, unlike the cotton mills. His manufacturing model was based on productivity, and he employed more skilled labour to create a superior product. This meant that he paid the best hourly rate, more than any other company in Birmingham; and this created enemies, keen to see their workforce living from hand to mouth on the breadline.

Why was he so philanthropic? Samuel knew what hard manual labour meant. Albert, his father, was a farmer who had no ambition. Under his stewardship, the farm was firmly in decline and its failure, mainly due to his lack of interest in it, made him a bitter and miserable man. By the time he was eight, his father was sometimes too drunk to get out of bed.

Samuel and his mother were working the farm alone. Winter and summer, they were up at four in the morning and worked until the sunset, or later if required. The work was exhausting, but it was the abuse they suffered under his father that damaged him the most. He vowed he would never touch alcohol. *There will be none of the demon drink for me.*

When he was sixteen, the frustration eventually erupted, and a rage engulfed him. One evening, an argumentative and ungrateful Albert wanted to throw his plate of hot food against the wall. As he raised his hand to launch it, the sixteen-year-old Samuel grabbed his arm, like the tongue of a hungry frog captures a fly, then he put the plate back down.

> "My labours put the food on this table father, and you will never throw another plate of it against the wall while I provide it. Is that clear?"

He never did it again, but he remained verbally abusive. Albert Hudson died, after a profuse round of drinking at the village pub, stumbling into the nearby canal and drowning alone in the dark water.

Samuel was eighteen when he inherited his father's property. He couldn't imagine living his life in a house that held all those terrible memories. Selling the farmstead immediately, with the profit made, he paid the remaining debt secured on it and bought a tiny cottage for his mother in a quaint village about twenty miles outside of Birmingham. Setting her up with a home, she would be safe and free to do as she wished. It was there that she would see out her days. On her sudden and unexpected passing, he invested the money back into his growing business.

Samuel, sensing he needed an education if he were to make his fledgling engineering business flourish further, approached a former private tutor, John Green, to instruct him.

John was a bright man with a good reputation. He accepted the post. For four years, during many evenings and on Sundays, John Green taught him everything he knew.

Since they had formed such a close bond, Samuel often smiled and wondered what his former tutor would say about Shilling. John Green was the closest thing Samuel would ever have to a proper father and John still nurtured him, even though the official tutoring days were far behind them.

By twenty-eight, Samuel was so deeply engrossed in his business that the thought of falling in love hadn't yet crossed his mind, even though he had developed into a handsome man. He was tall and well-built, possessed thick, brown wavy hair, a mischievous glint in his eye and an infectious smile. He was dignified in public but relaxed enough to be a little rough around the edges when at home. His most attractive feature was his sense of humour. When he laughed, he would tip his head back and give a roar of delight. No one could ever doubt his sincerity.

Samuel met Catherine Franco by accident one afternoon as he left his solicitor's office. Pressed for time, he barged out of the front door and onto the street. Without looking left or right, he ploughed into a young woman.

> "I am terribly sorry, Madam," he said apologetically. "I admit I was in such a rush that I didn't see you."

Instead of being enraged, she looked directly at him and gave a warm smile.

> "You are pardoned, Sir," she said. "I have done the same thing on several occasions and also had to apologise profusely."

To Samuel's dismay, he found himself staring at her—every inch of her, in fact. She wasn't a traditional English rose, but there was something beautiful about her. *She is exotic, exquisite even.*

Catherine had chestnut hair pinned up with a beautiful clasp. She had olive skin with the most delightful soft brown eyes, framed by delicately curled long lashes. Her voice sounded cultured. Her dress accentuated her figure beautifully. *Look at that magnificent smile, kind, yet commanding. She seems delightfully free-spirited, not in the slightest starchy and parochial. Quite a refreshing change, I must say.*

He liked her immediately, but he was confused. This confident man, who knew his way around the business world, had no idea about how to treat a lady, or even begin courting one. *I am going to need some help here.*

"May I introduce myself, Madam? My name is Samuel Hudson."

"Catherine Franco."

Her direct reply made her even more attractive to him. She extended her hand, a most irregular protocol for a lady. Samuel was starting to like her more and more.

Catherine scrutinised the young man in front of her. He was a refined gentleman but did not have the dialect of the upper classes. His dress was smart but not profligate. He lacked the grandeur that the elite displayed. *How curious—he isn't the slightest bit pretentious.*

Catherine realised Samuel was a little out of his depth, and contrary to all socially acceptable mores, boldly handed him her calling card.

Reassuringly gripping the valuable information, without a second thought, he asked if he could visit the following Sunday afternoon. She agreed. They settled on meeting at the tea house at Birmingham's elegant botanical gardens. There was no mention of a chaperone. Samuel wasn't a praying man, but he thanked whatever power maybe that seemed to be helping him.

Filled with a strange uninhibited affection, Samuel went directly to John Green to establish what had just happened.

10

BUT YOU DON'T DRINK, SAMUEL

As he had stayed at his tutor's home whilst he studied, when Samuel entered the joyously familiar house, it smelled like old books, dusty chalkboards and leather. The odours permeated the house, bringing back fond memories of the many hours he spent there filling his head with exciting new ideas.

On opening the door, Samuel advised John's house-keeper he'd find his own way to the study.

He knocked once and opened the door. John Green was bent over his desk, seemingly deep in thought. He looked up as his young student unexpectedly burst in.

"What on earth is the emergency, Sam? Have you got a problem at the factory? Do we need to solve an issue? Have you come to fetch me?"

John loved helping Sam solve technical problems at the foundry. Samuel had invested in very modern technology, and they spent a lot of time together, making the business run like clockwork, cracking the inevitable snags that cropped up with committed enthusiasm.

"No, John, everything at the factory is fine. It's—something else."

"Tea?"

"Whisky!" answered Samuel.

"You don't drink, Sam?"

John looked at him over his round spectacles.

"No, I don't drink, John." he concurred, but his body language confirmed he wanted one regardless.

John walked over to the walnut drinks cabinet and poured a little bit of whisky into a fine cut-crystal glass. He didn't pour too much—he was reasonably sure that Samuel would spit it out since he had no experience of the burning, golden liquid.

He handed his young student the drink and went back to the task on his desk, carefully inspecting a technical diagram. From the corner of his eye, John watched Samuel down the glass in a single gulp. Then he flopped into one of the well-worn leather chairs and sat looking at the fire, not flinching in the slightest.

"So, what is her name, Sam?" asked John without taking his eyes off the drawing.

Samuel was taken aback.

 "How do you know it's to do with a woman?"

The whisky was still burning his throat and had turned his stomach into a ball of fire. *I certainly won't be trying that again!*

"Well, Sam, there are only two things that make a sober man drink—love and loss."

Samuel Hudson would remember the words.

"John, I have met a wonderful young lady, a Miss Catherine Franco—and I am going to marry her."

"Ah, Sam, so you have met the fragrant—"

An impatient Samuel interrupted, in no mood for idle chit-chat.

"Yes, Miss Franco, and I am going to marry her."

"Does she know that yet, Sam?"

"No, but I am going to tell her on Sunday."

"Shouldn't you ask her first rather than simply tell her, Sam?"

"No. I was right the first time. This is far too important a matter to offer her a choice." he chuckled.

John did not even bother to question his rationale. He knew that it was useless to try and change Samuel's mind. Besides, he had never seen him so enamoured about a young lady, and he found his demeanour highly amusing to observe.

"So, it seems you know of her, John. Who is she?" asked his love-struck former pupil.

"Catherine Franco is the daughter of a Spanish diplomat. Her mother is British. Her parents are estranged after Josephine had an affair. At the time, it was a huge scandal. Carlo Franco went back to Madrid, and Josephine was living with her lover in India. To exacerbate the situation, Carlo Franco is Catholic and refuses to divorce his wife."

"Catholic?" said Samuel and rolled his eyes. "Are you trying to tell me in some sort of coded way that this will be difficult?"

"No, Sam, I am trying to tell you that there is a social stigma attached to this family. Yes, Catherine is about your age. However, she has no suitors, and she is a social pariah. For all her good breeding, and undeniable allure, nobody wants to marry her. Furthermore, she is politically minded. Women's suffrage, abolishing child labour, raising the lot of the poor, the works. If slavery was still allowed, she'd be against that too."

John paused to let the ideas sink in for a moment then continued with his cautionary advice.

"She is feisty and can cause tremendous ructions with a few offhand comments. You need to think very carefully, Samuel. This may affect your business. Society and the Catholic Church do not accept divorce even if it is her parents and not the young girl in question."

"John," he said, the twinkle was growing larger in his eye, "Catherine Franco sounds like the perfect partner."

John gave a resigned sigh. It was futile to argue with him.

10

MOVING TO THE COUNTRY AND BACK AGAIN

Samuel Hudson and Catherine Franco were married in the new Birmingham registry office, Edmund Street in 1846, a week after they met. They had no friends or family present, and the nuptials were witnessed by two secretaries. Even if her father could have attended, Catherine would have refused to be 'given away' by him, since she was not 'a possession'.

After the ceremony, Socrates took Samuel and Catherine back to his country house. Samuel gave his faithful assistant and the rest of the staff leave for seven days. The honeymooners spent a week alone in the countryside without another soul anywhere close to them.

Showing her experience, Catherine was clearly not a virgin, but it didn't perturb Samuel at all. She was a committed wife now, and he had her all to himself. He felt completely relaxed in her company. What began tenderly, culminated in a frenzy of passion. Catherine had no inhibitions. Samuel was insatiable. It was perfect.

They lay for hours entangled; her olive limbs entwined around him. He could not resist temptation and ran his hands delicately over her body, even while she slept. They laughed and played. They remained predominantly naked for the entire honeymoon, and after seven days of complete togetherness, they had no secrets. She was the woman of his dreams, and he was the fire of her nights.

With the honeymoon over, Samuel and Catherine returned to London. Samuel booked a suite at Claridge's. They intended that Catherine choose a cosy home there to settle in. He was doing more and more business in the city, so it was much more convenient than the country house outside Birmingham. John and his foreman, Jim Atherton, kept a close eye on production at the foundry, so he felt comfortable with his decision to spend time in both cities.

They chose a spacious townhouse in Mayfair, close to Hyde Park. Samuel allowed Catherine to decorate it as she wished. It had a striking Mediterranean style, vibrant colour, with an energy, an effervescence, absent in most British houses. But it wasn't the daring décor that brought soul to the house, it was Catherine. She filled it with laughter and joy. Her relationship with the staff was open and friendly. Her time in Spain, where day to day dealings with servants was different from those in Britain, influenced her behaviour in England.

Catherine, despite her approachability, had under the surface a lingering fieriness. On the rare occasions when her temper flared, she would rage at the staff, sometimes resorting to Spanish when she couldn't find the suitable vocabulary in English. Thankfully, as fast as she became angry, she softened, and an apology followed. On balance, her kindness and generosity endeared her to those who worked with her.

In social circles, they were an unpopular couple, and they loved it that way. Their friends were true, and they weren't bothered about the upper classes with their outward show of morality, yet with one foot always dipped in the depraved.

Catherine fell pregnant after a nail-biting fourteen months. The awful worry that she might be barren was over. Within days of hearing the good news, Samuel arrived at the Mayfair mansion with a brand new four-carat diamond ring of his choosing. As he slipped it onto her finger, he whispered:

"You are the love of my life, Catherine."

Unable to express her gratitude in words, Catherine simply stared into his eyes, gently let her eyelids close, then kissed him passionately, barely breaking to take a breath for quite some time.

Afterwards, he looked at the glittering diamond on her slim finger. He wanted to give her everything. Samuel was grateful for the fourteen months, but now he had, even more, to be thankful for. As he lay with her at the beginning of her pregnancy, he could feel her breasts become fuller, and her tummy harder. She suffered very little with side effects and was as passionate as always.

She chose the decorations for the nursery, interviewed nannies, and bought cute little clothes plus all the latest equipment designed to make mothering easier. Samuel allowed her an open budget, and she used it both with glee and a respectful restraint.

Soon, it was apparent that Catherine would have twins. Samuel employed the most qualified doctor, Dr Thomas Carr-Jackson, who worked in conjunction with the best midwife in London. There were frequent visits and tests to ensure the young mother and her precious babies were doing well.

11

CLEAN TOWELS AND CLEAN SHEETS

Catherine went into labour in the early morning of New Year's Eve. From the doorway, Samuel peered into the room to see how Catherine was faring. Doctor Carr-Jackson would walk over and say she was coping well.

By nine o'clock in the evening, Catherine was ready to deliver. Despite telling the expectant father that things were progressing to plan, after such a long labour, she was exhausted from the wait, the panic, the panting, the pushing and the pain. She was on the verge of unconsciousness. *The time for sparing Mr Hudson's feelings is over. He needs the truth.*

The doctor left the room and came into the hallway where an anxious Samuel marched to see him. Still tiptoeing around the subject, the physician said:

"Sir, may I speak candidly—"

Samuel noticed his crisp white apron now had blood on it.

"Out with it, man!" roared Samuel.

His aggression was very much out of character, although it was understandable he was impatient. Catherine's labour had been almost seventeen hours now.

"Sir, Mrs Hudson is exhausted. The babies are laying incorrectly—they're breeched—and we are struggling."

Samuel pushed past Dr Carr-Jackson and slammed open the bedroom door. The midwife spun round in shock and looked at him as he strode to be at Catherine's side.

For the first time in Samuel's existence, he had no control over a life-changing situation. He didn't understand what was happening and had no way of solving it.

"Catherine! Catherine, look at me!"

She barely opened her eyes—there was no energy left.

"Just one more push Catherine, just one more." urged the midwife.

Samuel wished with all his heart that his pent-up, panicked energy may be transferred into her body, to sustain her a little longer. At this point, he didn't care about the babies, only her.

With what must have been an act of the most tremendous will, Catherine screamed and gave the final push. She convulsed, then lay still. The doctor took her wrist, then a grave countenance fell on his face. *There is no heartbeat.*

Moments later, the first baby emerged, bottom first. The doctor pulled out the rest of the lump of grisly lifeless flesh. Blood started to seep from Catherine and soak into the towels beneath her. The second baby was pulled out, its head appearing first. Following it came so much blood—enough to soak half the entire bed's linen. The two dead infants lay between Catherine's legs, blue and stiff. Catherine's face was pain-free at last. The midwife lowered her nightdress to cover her, then reached towards the babies.

"Sir—" said the remorseful doctor.

"Get out!" thundered Samuel.

A fierce, defensive Socrates sent the doctor and midwife from the room.

"Get out! Move! Faster!" he yelled.

Socrates left the bedroom with them, closing the door behind him. Within earshot of all the commotion, by now, the worried staff had gathered at the bottom of the hall-way.

What they heard would remain with them forever. A growl came from behind the closed door. It was like the sound of an animal in pain. Then came a scream that seemed to last for an eternity. In fact, Samuel screamed until he was hoarse. Then he sobbed in desperation. It was the sound of a man in abject pain.

Samuel stayed alone in the room for two hours. Socrates did not leave his watch post, which was just outside the door.

When Samuel emerged, he had his jacket off. His white shirttails hung over his trousers, also splashed in congealed blood. His hair was unkempt, his eyes were red. He did not—or could not—speak.

He walked down the hallway. Socrates could hear the study door slam behind him. He braced himself and entered the bedroom, feeling unprepared for the terrible sight that lay ahead of him.

He was stunned. The scene that greeted him was serene. The bloodied sheets had been stripped from the bed, rolled in a ball and hidden behind a chair. Catherine had been washed. Her hair flowed beautifully around her head and neck. A pristine, but lifeless, angelic baby lay in each arm, and a fresh, clean white sheet laid over them all.

12

THE REQUEST FOR A PECULIAR GIFT

Miss Annabelle's features had softened over the years. She was still stunning. Mercifully, the hardship she had experienced earlier in life had not changed that. Now though, when her smile met her eyes, they crinkled at the corners when she laughed.

She never let Shilling out of her sight for a minute. She even learned to horse ride, so she could accompany Samuel and his daughter when they went riding in Hyde Park. The little girl was a natural rider and had full command of her pony. The staff in the house were delighted when Annabel and Shilling first arrived in the kitchen to show them their new riding gear.

The kitchen was a wonderful place for a young girl. Cook always had a treat hidden somewhere, and after riding, it was the best place to be. In winter there was the warm fire and a hot mug of cocoa, or alternatively lashings of cold, refreshing homemade lemonade in summer.

The house was full of love once more. There was always excitement and always something to celebrate. Life was to be enjoyed not endured Mr Hudson frequently reminded them.

Samuel had no qualms with Shilling befriending the servants, after all, he was just a farmer's son from the backwoods of the Midlands, and he wanted her to know that all people deserved respect.

He also taught her to share. At Christmases and birthdays, they made a huge fuss, and everyone who worked in the house received a modest present. Even though it took a lot of patience on the part of Samuel and Miss Annabelle, they allowed Shilling to assist in choosing the gifts. On the big day, they would meet in the dining room where cook would put out tea and Christmas cake for everybody, and then they would open their presents.

At first, all the staff were taken aback by Samuel's generosity, but thanks to their unwavering support, he saw them as the extended family he never had.

More importantly, Samuel was happy. Shilling was a joy to the house as she tore through it on one or other mission, usually followed by Socrates. They were a dangerous pair, always getting into humorous scrapes. Socrates adored the gloriously excitable little girl, and she twisted him around her little finger. This resulted in many an adventure that Miss Annabelle would never have agreed to if she had known the full details in advance.

As always, Samuel went to see Shilling in the evenings in the schoolroom. These days, she was usually sitting at a table when he arrived, playing with a train set that she had chosen at the toy shop. She loved watching the wheels spin round, especially when her father told her inquisitive mind how his factory made the wheels for real trains.

"Miss Annabelle."

He always started his conversations with her this way.

"Hello, Samuel," she smiled.

"How are my beautiful ladies today?"

Annabelle gave a bemused look as Samuel playfully raised his eyebrows. The most delightful, contagious laugh emerged from his throat. Annabelle couldn't help but chuckle. It was then, a wholly absorbed Shilling looked up to see her Papa, briefly pausing her play with the little toy train.

"Oh Annabelle," he joked, "do you have a doll for Shilling to play with?"

Shilling looked up horrified.

"No, Sir" she replied, not grasping the teasing going on. "Shilling has no desire to play with dolls of any kind—she always reminds me she wants to play with trains."

"Now, what are we going to do about that, Annabelle?" murmured a pensive Samuel.

She could barely hear him. He mouthed the words as if they were only meant for him to hear. He had recognised a passion in his daughter and was clearly working out how to capture and cultivate it, just like his mother had chosen to teach him about the farming implements.

Samuel sat down in his regular chair in front of the fire. The love of having supper with Shilling and Annabelle every evening never lost its sparkle. In the schoolroom, there was a small dining table, surrounded by three chairs. Together, they would sit and merrily share a meal and tell each other about the day's events.

Shilling's day consisted mostly of walks, riding, school and playing. Annabelle accompanied her throughout. After dinner, Samuel and Shilling would sit together in the big comfortable chair next to the fire. Shilling would climb onto her father's lap, wiggle herself into the warm crook of his arm, and they would discuss whatever topic was on Shilling's mind that day. Then, he would read her a story, always an adventure story. Annabelle would sit on the other armchair and listen, revelling in how warm and cosy they were together.

"Papa—" asked Shilling clearly angling for something. "Do you remember that we went to the toy shop the other day? I have decided I want that special red steam engine for my birthday. The one that works with real fire, Papa. Did you know it gives out tiny puffs of actual smoke as it moves? It is quite a thing to observe."

"Shilling, my darling," said Samuel in the gentle voice that Annabelle loved, "you are still too small for that engine. One day when you are a big girl, you can have all the trains that you want, and you may even name one after yourself."

"Oh, Papa, that will take forever."

Her little green eyes flashed with begging disappointment.

"I am not too small, Papa. Very soon, I will be seven. You did say earlier that I am a big girl now."

Samuel laughed. *Indeed, I did say it, and now she is using that to negotiate an outcome.*

"Or perhaps, we can go to your factory in Birmingham again and see the real ones?"

"Of course, Shilling, and we will take Miss Annabelle with us."

"Oh, yes, Papa. Miss Annabelle has never seen a real train before."

"Yes, she has, Shilling," chuckled Samuel, "and one day, we will name one after her as well."

The little child spoke less and less. She began yawning and rubbing her eyes.

"Are you tired, Shilling?" Samuel asked gently, then looked down.

Shilling was already asleep.

Samuel sat with the small girl in his arms for a long time. He was never in a rush to put her to bed. He would watch her breathe, marvel at the seamless skin that covered her face like silk, touch her little pink fingers and study the black eyelashes.

He looked at his daughter. *Oh, how lucky I am*. For a moment, emotion overwhelmed him, and he choked back the tears. He had got a second chance at happiness so immense he felt his heart could burst. *Not everyone is that blessed.*

Annabelle sat next to Samuel and studied him. She swallowed hard. When she watched him like this, deep in himself, contented, she had to fight back the emotion. Her poor little baby would have been the same age as Shilling. *Come on now. Chin up. There's no point wondering what she might have become, you'll only upset yourself again. What's done is done.* Tonight though, her thoughts would not be so easily extinguished. She felt a crushing tightness in her chest and throat. Samuel took Shilling and gently put her into her warm, clean, downy bed. A comforting smell of dried lavender posies filled the air. Annabelle went back to the table and started putting the toys away.

Samuel returned, but it took a while before he spoke.

"Miss Annabelle," he said softly, "it is not too late to start a family of your own, you know."

"What do you mean, Sam?" she asked, hesitant to discuss the subject.

"Annabelle, you have looked after Shilling tirelessly for many years now. Surely you must have a yearning to have your own child?"

"I am too afraid." She answered candidly, "I am too afraid to love again. It's the pain, Sam. It hurt so much to lose them. Martin fell ill and a few days later my beautiful baby Sarah got it, cholera, and they—"

She took a deep, steadying breath through her nose, then continued in a matter of fact way.

"—Well, they died. It was as if they never really existed, as if they were only in my imagination. If Socrates had not come to fetch me that day, I am sure would have thrown myself under the hooves of a horse within days. More than anything else, I wanted to die and be with them."

After all those years spent together, she was finally telling Samuel her painful story in full. She didn't dare to say to him all the details, but she felt secure enough to reveal the anguish that still haunted her in the darker hours.

> "Nobody will ever know what it felt like. To lose a partner is devastating, but no one should ever feel this pain of losing a child."

My dearest Annabelle, I know all too well the road down which you have travelled. Her divulgence made tears well in her eyes. One at a time, large round teardrops spilt down her face, after sharing as much as she could for the moment. She stopped talking, her soul yearning for that happy time in her life, now closed off forever. Her sobs grew in strength. She flopped down into one of the armchairs.

Wanting to offer some solace, Samuel sat on the side of the seat and hesitantly put his arm around her, wanting to shield her from the pain. Her arms stayed firmly stuck to her lap, her hands clutching a cold, drenched handkerchief. He held her like that for a long time.

Nobody would ever know how badly Samuel needed the touch of another woman at that moment. It would have been easy to kiss her, maybe more, but that would be taking advantage of her vulnerability, making it thoroughly inappropriate for him, despite his physical attraction. Even in this intense moment, he knew that it would be cruel to take things further and that he would regret it if he did.

"You are right, Annabelle," he said kindly stroking her hair and wiping away the last of the tears. "Nobody should ever feel that pain."

He held her a little longer, then he kissed her sweetly on the top of her head, before wishing her good night and leaving the room.

13

MEETING JOHN GREEN
IN LONDON

It was 1856 and a joyous, important day—Shilling's birthday. Samuel and Socrates were waiting in the carriage outside the front door of the Mayfair townhouse. At precisely three o'clock, the front door opened, and Miss Annabelle escorted Shilling down the steps.

Shilling looked charming in a pale blue dress. She had a small bead-encrusted bag dangling from her wrist and wore a long white fur coat which was buttoned up to her chin. She sported a white fur hat to match, and it trapped the snowflakes as they gently drifted around her. Her long hair had curls that reached to well below her shoulders. It was not tied up; it was pinned back from her face with a beautiful silver comb in the shape of a butterfly. Samuel had bought the comb on one of his trips abroad. He saw it displayed in the window of a jewellery store in Paris. The one in the window would be way too big for the little girl, so he had a miniature made for her. When he collected it, he invested in the full-size one too for when she was older. *Her wedding day, perhaps?*

Her skin was fair, but it was the emerald green eyes with dark lashes that won attention. From the youngest age, her eyes were the barometer of her mood. When she was angry, she would toss her head back, her dark hair would sway, and her eyes would open wide. All hellfire would shoot out of them—or so Samuel thought when he watched her. He often had to hide a smile or stifle a laugh when Shilling was petulant. *I rather like the confident contrarian streak she has inherited from me. It will serve her well, I am sure.*

Socrates assisted her into the couch as if she was royalty and Shilling gave a peel of laughter when he bowed and flourished.

"Good afternoon, Madame."

"Oh Socrates, you are teasing me," giggled Shilling.

"And where may we be taking you to today, young lady?"

"Sir, I am going to Claridge's with my Papa."

"Ah, Claridge's, you say?"

"Yes, to celebrate, remember? Papa and I are going to meet Mr Green for high tea. Tell me you haven't forgotten my birthday, Socrates?"

"No, Miss Shilling, my dear, how can I forget your birthday? You remind me of the date and your plans all the time."

Samuel put his head back and laughed. *No, I'll definitely not forget that strange but fortuitous day either.*

Shilling moved closer to Samuel, and he placed a blanket over her little legs as she snuggled next to him.

"Papa, I've never been to a hotel before. What's it like? Are there a lot of people? Where do you eat? What can you have? Do people really sleep there? How will Mr Green find us? Can Socrates come too?"

The barrage of questions didn't stop, and the carriage hadn't even moved yet.

Within minutes, Samuel Hudson's cab arrived at the luxurious Mayfair hotel's doors. Its owner had recently bought and redeveloped four neighbouring buildings and expanded the well-appointed smaller property into a fabulous new construction. The smartly dressed commissionaire complete with an eye-catching gold-braided top hat, stepped forward to open the door and assisted Shilling out of the carriage. Greeting her, he announced politely:

"Good afternoon, Miss."

"Good afternoon, Sir," she replied with an infectious, confident smile.

The commissionaire ushered Samuel and Shilling into the lobby. There were impressive, glistening crystal chandeliers, gleaming black and white marble floors, and a monumental curving staircase, with a gilt-edged bannister. The whole place was buzzing with people.

As they walked into the hotel, time stopped for a moment. It seemed that everybody turned to look at them, and for a few seconds nobody moved. *So, this is the enigmatic Samuel Hudson.*

They watched a very handsome man holding the hand of a beautiful little girl. Samuel was dressed in an understated black suit. His white shirt was crisp, and his shoes perfectly polished.

He wasn't known to patronise social gatherings often, so this unusual appearance would undoubtedly get a mention in the society column of the Times.

Several people paced over to greet him, but he excused himself politely explaining that it was his daughter's special day and he would be lavishing all his attention upon her. Everyone smiled respectfully, but if they knew Samuel better, they would also have known this was his way of dismissing them graciously. He had no time for the 'polite' duplicitous Victorian society, straitlaced when out but thoroughly immoral in private.

He held Shilling's hand tightly, not trusting anyone near her. He spotted John Green sitting in the lounge and walked over to him. John stood up and shook hands with Samuel, then turned to say:

"Good afternoon, Shilling."

"Oh, hello, Uncle John! Papa said that you would meet us here! Did it take you long to get here? How long are you staying? What do you think of the place? Did you know that it is my birthday today?"

I bet from this moment until she falls asleep in the carriage, Shilling won't stop talking—or the incessant questioning.

They were seated at a round table and chairs that were covered in beautiful regency-striped material of red and pink. John gave her the birthday present he had chosen but made her promise not to open it until she got home. It was a futile exercise, and within minutes, Shilling had torn off the wrapping paper.

Samuel didn't give a damn if she opened it at the table. The people could stare if they wished. He had enough money to buy the hotel if he wanted, and no one would tell him to stifle his daughter's joy. Shilling squealed when she saw the steam engine. *It really was the one. The fabulous red one. The one that burnt minute pieces of coal smaller than a penny—and best of all, the one that puffed real smoke.*

In her own little world pushing the train along, Shilling was barely distracted when the teapot, cups and saucers arrived with their familiar chinking sound. She did squeal with delight when she saw the exquisite afternoon tea trolley roll by, burgeoning with intricate pastries, delicate finger sandwiches and sumptuous slices of iced cake, all beautifully made. She sat at the table like a little lady holding court with her father, a man who simply adored her. Shilling hardly noticed the finery of the venue, which amused John. She said 'it was pretty, but Papa's house was even better'.

"Samuel, have you thought about the next step in Shilling's education? I notice that she may be taking after you in the engineering department?" enquired John, with a cheeky smile, watching the young girl navigate the obstacles on the table with the toy train.

"Yes," said a pensive Samuel. "It has been on my mind. By her eighth birthday, I would like her to be following a set curriculum. She will need a full-time governess. I will choose somebody suitable, and Annabelle will oversee the day to day management of it. I trust her, she always puts Shilling's interests first."

"Ah yes, Sam, how is Miss Annabelle?"

"She bides well. I simply don't know what we would do without her. She and Socrates are the cornerstones of the household."

"You do know that Shilling will need to be introduced to London society at some point?" said John cautiously.

"John, I won't trudge Shilling from party to party and instil in her the belief that her only worth is a beautiful face or a large fortune. I want Shilling to be her own person to follow her own dream."

"Sam, you can't create another—Catherine—"

Oh, dear. Have I gone too far? Said too much? To John's relief, Samuel took the comment from the well-meant place where it came. He trusted John and knew that he cared for both of them.

"Catherine," whispered Samuel quietly.

For a moment, noticeably tinged with sadness, he stared, in his usual wistful, bittersweet way when her name was mentioned.

Just as suddenly as it darkened, his mood brightened, he smiled as the cogs in his mind returned to happier thoughts, and he laughed, sure of what his next move should be.

"John, you and I are going to allow Shilling to create herself. I know my daughter, and she is a bonny, confident little girl and one day she will be a fine woman. We shall give her a sound basic education, and let her choose her direction."

Shilling had had fun, but now, as she fidgeted noisily, it was a sign it was time to go. Her tummy was full, and her mind was on her steam train, the nugget of coal from which she had not yet been allowed to light. *I need to see the smoke. That is the whole point.*

"Uncle John, are you staying at the hotel tonight?" asked Shilling politely.

"Actually, Shilling, I will be staying at your house this evening."

Shilling hopped from one leg to another as she begged:

"Uncle John, can we set up the engine when we get home, please?"

"Of course,!" answered John Green with as much enthusiasm as Shilling asked the question.

He was exhausted with her whirlwind energy, but what was an uncle for if not to spoil her.

The maître d' ushered the three of them politely into the foyer. John was carrying the steam engine, and Samuel was helping Shilling put on her coat. About to exit the lobby, Samuel heard someone greet him by name, and he turned around to see fellow industrialist Sir Charles Buckingham behind him.

"Sir Charles—I'm afraid I can't stop," said Samuel as he shook his hand, his cheerful expression betraying his inner thoughts of contempt.

Sir Charles Buckingham owned a massive foundry that was in direct opposition to Samuel's factory. He delighted in trying to poach Samuel's clients with all sorts of wild promises, but they were still loyal to their dependable supplier. The few who did choose to do some business with Sir Charles would return to support Samuel after being disappointed with the quality of the products eventually shipped to them. Charles was an odious man, happy to cut corners on workmanship and the workplace to line his pockets with even more profit.

Samuel's righteous attitude always irked Sir Charles, and so, he had developed an equally off-handed manner toward him when they met in public. It was only the rules of polite society that made the fake 'pleasantries' necessary.

Samuel had never liked the man if he were honest. Like his father, he was a hard drinker with continual rumours of his cruelty and abuse toward his staff, particularly the women and children. Samuel ignored most of the tittle-tattle, but he could not shake off the fundamental distaste he felt in the crude man's company.

John and Shilling greeted Sir Charles politely, then with John knowing the true nature of the industrialists' rancorous relationship, excused the two of them. They headed toward the carriage, leaving Samuel alone with his competitor.

"Ah, Samuel! Visiting Claridge's. Trying to break into society, I see."

Samuel ignored his barbed comment.

"You must be overwhelmed by all that splendour, Samuel, since you were a lowly, unfortunate farm boy not so long ago. Perhaps I can invite you for dinner at my private club sometime? Show you how it is done, dear boy?"

"No, thank you, Charles," Samuel smiled. "I prefer to spend my time at home."

The return was short and to the point. Sir Charles was more furious over the omission of his title of 'Sir' in the response than the rejection of the invitation.

"You are committing a sizeable business blunder, Mr Hudson. You're missing out on lucrative opportunities with my fellow industrialists with this enforced solitary confinement of yours. Take Webster and Horsfall, for instance. They pooled their resources and are now supplying miles of telegraph cables that lie beneath the sea, connecting the world. With the expansion in the railways, we could make a killing."

"I am just a farm boy, Charles, surely you don't want to work with a lowly person like me! I remain convinced you'll be better off with one of those well to do industrialist friends of yours."

Samuel tipped his hat in a farewell gesture and headed for his carriage.

Shilling was already asleep, and John was relieved there had been a temporary ceasefire with her questioning.

Socrates brought Samuel some tea to the study and John poured himself a whisky. They were both tired after the day spent with the loveable if overly excited birthday girl.

"That child is a blessing in your life, Sam," said John.

"Yes, indeed she is. She has taught me that there is more to life than working."

"Things are all good at the forge with our existing operations, Sam, but you may need to come up for a month or so to supervise the new project we are working on."

"Yes, I was going to talk to you about that. My household staff here all need some time off, so I will spend a month in Birmingham. Miss Annabelle can see to Shilling and Socrates will be with me of course. Can you please remind me to arrange a cook and a housekeeper for the country house? We can stay there."

"Of course." said John "Changing the subject, Sam, what was Charles Buckingham on about, earlier?"

"He didn't say very much of any consequence, John. He was just his usual charming self."

"It is strange, John. When they passed the Reform Bill in 1832, one would have thought that the upper classes would learn some respect for their workers. The aristocracy are broke, the gentry are becoming unnecessary. One of these days, industrialisation will create so many jobs that no one will want to work on their land. You know I was a farm boy, John. Luckily, we owned our small piece of land, but many like us didn't have that privilege. When are the selfish laggards going to realise that their world has changed?"

"Those with old money have no respect for the industrialists, Samuel. It's always been the same since Henry VIII upset everything, selling the monastery land to the wealthy merchants. The blue-bloods have had a bee in their bonnets about the rise of the common man ever since."

"God forbid that I earn the aristocracy's respect," he replied. "They have no morals."

14

TAMING MISS WALLACE

Miss Wallace, Shilling's governess, was in Samuel's study. Her nose was in the air, and her upper-class voice was doing its best to throw a tantrum.

"Mr Hudson!" she berated, her voice an octave higher than usual.

She was about to have her usual tirade against his 'uncontrollable' daughter. He had heard it before, and all he wanted to do was escape the woman, but she had him trapped in his own study, and he was unable to find a polite reason to leave.

"Yes, Miss Wallace?" Samuel sighed.

"Mr Hudson, Shilling is refusing to cooperate with me. Heaven help me, I have been her governess for several years now, and I no longer have the reserves to tolerate her lack of compliance."

"Compliance? Again?" he replied with his elbows on his desk and his head between his hands.

"Yes, compliance."

Samuel lifted his head and sat up in his chair, trying very hard to get comfortable enough so that he could concentrate fully on the tiresome confrontation.

"Mr Hudson, I am at the end of my tether. Shilling displays no interest in any academic subjects appropriate to the education of a young lady. She refuses to read anything romantic, has no interest in poetry, yawns through Shakespeare— "

"—Have you asked her what she would prefer to read?" interrupted Samuel.

"Yes, she insists upon visiting the most modern book shops with the latest publications. She is choosing books written by authors that I have never heard of. Jules Verne? Who is this author for heaven's sake? Or Edgar Alan Poe. All the gothic horror nonsense from Mary Shelley, really? She pens the most immoral novels."

"If Shilling shows an interest in them, I am happy to purchase the books. You must respect her wishes to enrich her mind, within reason, of course. I will ask Socrates to collect them for you."

"That is not the point, Mr Hudson. She says that she is bored with arithmetic and wants to study absurdly complicated algebra and geometry. This is not fit for a young lady. What man will ever want to marry a woman who is unable to converse on the same level as the upper class or is more attracted to the sciences than he maybe?"

"Miss Wallace, I am not educating Shilling to be a wife, mother or a socialite. I support her choices. If she finds Emily Bronte tedious, well, so do I!"

"That is not all, she refuses to do embroidery. She appreciates music and opera but will not participate in it no matter how hard I try. If I ask her to draw, she draws machines or technical plans. Her 'fine art' is a preposterous amalgamation of loud colour."

The grind of having this conversation yet again meant Miss Wallace's energy was beginning to wane, and now she was speaking in her normal voice.

"Her greatest heroes are Leonardo Da Vinci, Isaac Newton and the horrendous atheist Charles Darwin. And then there's the astronomer Caroline Herschel, the mathematician Ada Lovelace. It is not only her mind that I am concerned about, but also her soul. She won't go to church either."

"Miss Wallace, Shilling is fourteen, and the world is changing at a rapid pace. Shilling has an enquiring mind, and I cannot stifle it and insist that she read novels written by some dire romantics stuck in the world of the cart and horse when we are already moving towards mechanisation. You may be stuck in a rut, Miss Wallace, but the world is not. I am educating my daughter to grow and move forward—with it."

"But—but—" Miss Wallace stuttered, "what about her spiritual growth, Mr Darwin represents hell itself."

"Oh, my dear Miss Wallace, hell is sitting in a classroom all day bored to death by what you are forced to study. As an educator, please tell me, where is the sense in crushing another person's eager, enquiring mind?"

The dismayed governess had no reply. She pursed her lips, put her aloof nose in the air as usual and waited for him to dismiss her. There was to be no relief just yet. Samuel's playful eyes began to twinkle.

"How do you think she would cope in a finishing school? Think of all the social airs and graces that could be instilled into her there. I believe a few have been set up in America. There is talk of them starting in Switzerland too."

Miss Wallace lacked a sense of humour and didn't reply. Sensing it was time to show some leadership, Samuel attempted to ease her mind after his flippancy.

"Let me give the situation some thought, please. Annabelle will discuss it with Shilling too. You may go now."

With that, a slightly less irked governess returned to her work.

That evening, Samuel, Miss Annabelle and Shilling had dinner together in the schoolroom. He insisted that his talkative daughter be quiet during the meal, or they would never leave the table. He said with a wink:

"Shilling, after dinner, you will have my full attention, right now, I need to finish my supper to have enough energy to listen to you."

Throughout their customary post-dinner cup of tea. Samuel and Annabelle would listen, and Shilling would do the talking. Since Annabelle had been in every school lesson since Shilling was five, thereby gaining an education too, she had no shortage of wisdom or knowledge to share. She regularly surprised Samuel with her observations.

Samuel tried to answer all Shilling's questions to the best of his ability but realised that his daughter's extensive interests were beginning to overtake his own knowledge on occasions. In fact, he realised that it was time that he caught up with what was happening in the world of science.

An idea popped into his mind, but he felt he would first consult with Annabelle before he told Shilling. When it came to his daughter, Annabelle always played a significant role in his decision-making processes. She accepted Shilling like her own and her choices were based on a genuine love for the girl. This surrogate maternal loyalty enabled Samuel to trust her judgement on the most important or sensitive of issues.

It was bedtime for Shilling. She kissed Samuel good night.

"I love you, Papa," she yawned.

"I love you too, Shilling," Samuel smiled,

"Annabelle, if you are agreeable," said Samuel, "please stay a while, I need to talk to you."

Samuel loved to spend some evenings sitting and talking with Annabelle after Shilling's bedtime. Socrates would provide another pot of tea at about eleven o'clock, and they would have a piece of cook's cake of the day, then retire to their beds.

Just like with Socrates, Sam had developed a warm friendship with her. She had grown comfortable in his presence. They would play backgammon or cards to while away the hours. Annabelle proved to be a superb gambler, and she beat Sam at cards hands down. This caused endless banter between the staff. They began betting on the games in secret. Samuel was suspicious of Socrates's on-going curiosity as to whom had won the night before until he heard him discussing the betting

odds with Lizzy. Samuel had a good chuckle and nev
on that he knew what they were up to.

"Miss Wallace was in my study earlier, Annabelle. It's the same as always, Shilling is not applying herself to the planned curriculum. Her interests extend to the most obscure subjects, and now she is reading Darwin."

"I am sorry she is reading The Origin of Species. I didn't think that it would offend you."

"It doesn't offend me—it offends Miss Wallace!"

Samuel chuckled loudly at her comment.

"I see it as an indication of how important science is in her understanding of the world. Where does Shilling see these books? Where is her curiosity fed?"

"Well, Sam, we visit all the bookshops in London, and she listens to the academics speaking to each other when we go to libraries and coffee shops. Books are more like educated friends to her than mere objects. She also has a pen friend at an American university in Massachusetts. She pretends to be a boy, so he will reply. At first, I was against these contrarian practices, but it is so difficult to get information these days if you are a woman, so I allowed it to continue. Sometimes they even refuse to sell certain books to women. We send Socrates to get them."

"Do you have a list of titles she is interested in?" asked Sam.

"Yes—and, of course, that list of hers is frighteningly long."

"I will place an order for whatever she wants. Let's have Socrates collect them all to make sure we get everything."

"What will Miss Wallace say?"

"Miss Wallace must continue with her foundation curriculum, but Shilling may read what she wishes to extend her understanding of the world we live in."

There was a natural lull in the conversation, with Samuel deep in thought and Annabel continuing with her needlework. *I have to tell her what's on my mind.*

"Annabelle, I want to take Shilling to Paris," he announced, relaxed now, lounging in a comfortable chair, "—and I want you to come with us. And Socrates."

In her wildest dreams, Annabelle had never anticipated going somewhere so magical.

"Paris! Oh yes, Sam, Shilling will love it. I will love it. Of course, I would delight in travelling with you."

She did not cease smiling for almost an hour and only stopped when she finally fell asleep.

15

THE JOURNEY TO FRANCE

It was the summer of 1864 when Samuel and Shilling arrived in the glamourous French capital around noon, after their long overnight rail and sea journey. They were accompanied by Annabelle and Socrates both secretly ecstatic about the sojourn. It was warm, but the sky was overcast, and there was some light drizzle. No one cared. From the moment they left the train carriage, the sights, sounds and smells of Paris were utterly beguiling.

Shilling, now nearly fifteen thought this was the most exciting experience she had ever had. She was a young lady who looked a little older than her real age. Very little of Shilling's outwardly delicate appearance had changed, apart from her height. Her father thought she was as beautiful now as when she was a little girl.

Her face had a little matured, her limbs were long and wiry, awaiting womanhood to round them and her already dark hair had become darker yet. More than once, Samuel had seen young men staring at her. It put him in a bad mood for the rest of the day. None of them would be good enough for her in his eyes.

Shilling didn't enjoy fussy clothes any more than her father did, and was enjoying the latest fashion of less full 'walking' skirts. She found crinoline was terribly awkward to wear, even something as simple as sitting down posed a problem.

Samuel loved her enquiring mind, boundless energy, and a boldness that men told him bordered on arrogance. Samuel really didn't care what men thought. If Shilling intimidated them with her knowledge, he was not going to apologise for that. He was a self-made man and would not put unnecessary obstacles in the path of his daughter's future, for the sake of mere convention, especially if it were more 'for show' than sound reason.

Samuel had made reservations for them at the Grand Hotel du Louvre, the most modern hotel in Paris. The reviews of the place were bordering on otherworldly. Boasting seven hundred rooms, featuring ground breaking levels of comfort, with lifts and wide staircases, this magnificent place had to be seen to be believed.

No less than twelve hundred and fifty employees worked there daily, providing countless services to guests for the first time: omnibus transport to and from the train stations, personal city guides, interpreters, an information desk and a foreign exchange bureau. The restaurant also acquired an international reputation, because, on top of regional French fare, it was the first to offer the most famous dishes from a variety of countries.

He had chosen a large suite to accommodate them. Huge China urns stood alongside the doorways, and every available surface had vases of flowers placed upon them. The crystal, silver and gold vessels proudly held aloft the scented blooms of roses, lilies, peonies, tulips and cultivars Samuel could not identify.

The large sitting room was filled with beautiful fine French furniture, perfect to the last detail, but the bedrooms were the most beautiful. Each one was decorated in the Rococo style with gilt scrolls, silk coverings and oriental rugs. The four-poster beds stretched to the high ceilings. Yards and yards of silk brocade hung resplendently from them. The renaissance art displayed on the walls were hand painted works from the studios of famous masters. If they wanted to spend time together, there was a sitting room with a welcoming fireplace.

They had the option to have their meals in their suite or take them in the hotel dining room. They chose to do both. Socrates had the duty of ordering room service if anyone desired refreshments. Samuel allocated Miss Annabelle the beautiful pink bedroom, which was the best one in the suite.

Shilling couldn't have cared less about the colour of her bedroom or the silk on the beds. Naturally, she did pay attention to tea and pastries served in the room at three o'clock. For Shilling, though, there was something far more exciting to contemplate.

"Where are you going this time, Shilling?" asked a puzzled Samuel.

It was the third time in that hour that she was leaving the suite. It was making her father anxious. They were usually inseparable, which was for the best. He feared Shilling's precocious demeanour, coupled with looking older than her age, might inevitably lead her into trouble.

"Papa, I am on my way to the lounge, the music is so beautiful, and the hotel is so grand, and—"

"Shilling, you will not leave this suite unaccompanied again, do you understand me?"

"But Papa, when did you ever care about rules?"

"Shilling, you are a young lady now. We are in a foreign country where you can barely speak the language, and it is for your own safety. If you get into difficulties, there is no telling how it might end. Tomorrow, we will begin exploring more of the city. Let us rest today after the long journey."

Shilling sat on a luxuriously carved Louis XVI style chair, clearly sulking.

"You do know Miss Wallace has been teaching me French?"

From the corner of his eye, he saw Socrates shake his head at her to warn her not to challenge her father's wisdom. Samuel ignored her protests and soon she gave up with her petulance.

After a few minutes, Shilling went to sit next to her father on the sofa. Samuel was reading a newspaper and Shilling feigned interest in the pages.

"Alright then, Shilling, what do you want to tell me?" sighed Samuel, with a warm smile, never able to lose his temper with her for long.

"Well, Papa," she began, "earlier I was riding in the 'moving floor'. I believe it may be called a 'lift' or 'elevator'. It is quite something. It is a compartment that travels between the hotel's different levels in a unique vertical tunnel within the building."

Her enthusiasm in the concept was visibly blossoming the more she spoke.

"Do you know, Papa, that this is the first hotel in the whole world that has one—no, two—of these lifts! And have you heard what else—"

She didn't wait to find out if he knew.

"—They are driven by a steam engine. Can you imagine that grimy black workhorse, rumbling away inside a spectacular hotel like this? Papa, I want to see it. Socrates was going to ask the concierge, but he hasn't had the time, and I so wanted to see it working—which is why I was going to find it myself. It was designed by a gentleman called Otis Tufts who—."

"For goodness sake, Shilling, just once can't you be like other girls who are only interested in hats and clothes?" replied her father, both half-joking, and half-exhausted.

"But, Papa!"

Shilling was ready for a debate, although she didn't need to be.

"Of course, I'll arrange for us to see this magnificent invention. Why didn't you just ask me?"

Shilling stifled a giggle. Miss Annabelle shook her head, and Samuel gave Socrates a wink.

The month in Paris was passing quickly. Every sunrise brought forth a new adventure. They met in the breakfast room at nine o'clock daily to plan their sightseeing. They would walk or go by carriage to whichever attraction they wanted to see.

Shilling enjoyed the Paris Salon, but she was more intrigued by the enormous sculptures than the paintings. On visiting Notre Dame, when Samuel explained how old the building was and what tools they used to build it, Shilling fired a barrage of questions at him, and he made a mental note to buy her a book on cathedral building in the Middle Ages on their return.

They would lunch at a restaurant or café and then take a slow walk through the parks and gardens of the picturesque French capital. Then, they would rest in the suite until seven o'clock, when it would be time for their evening meal in the dining room, or in situ if they preferred.

Samuel sometimes booked a show for them after dinner, either the ballet or opera. Shilling had stated firmly that she didn't enjoy the opera, but Samuel saw her choke back tears after watching a performance of La Traviata as Violetta died in Alfredo's arms. He enjoyed the peace of the late evening when they finally retired to the suite. He was mentally exhausted after a day with Shilling, more so in this new exotic location, which fuelled even more intense bouts of questioning.

Most nights, Shilling went to bed when they returned late to the suite. Samuel and Annabelle sat in front of the fire, staring at its vibrant flames dancing against the dark sooty backdrop. She often curled up on the sofa with her embroidery, and he lounged in a comfortable chair. Socrates always felt compelled to explore the Parisian nightlife once his daily duties were complete. He would politely announce his departure:

"I trust that is everything, Sir? Have a good evening."

"Enjoy yourself, Socrates. Just one thing—don't get arrested for being drunk and disorderly."

"Sir, the French are permanently drunk. They drink wine from dawn until dusk—actually, no, until dawn! I am sure there will be no problem—I will blend in perfectly."

Samuel chuckled at his parting comment.

He poured a cup of tea for himself and Annabelle. His shirt sleeves were rolled up to the elbows, his collar was unbuttoned, and his shirttails hung over his trousers. She smiled when she saw him. He would always be a farm boy at heart.

Annabelle was relaxing, reclining on the sofa wearing a comfortable French ankle-length dressing gown, which she said was the latest fashion. It was white with delicate lace and draped around her comfortably. Doing his best not to look, he could still see the outline of her pale, shapely body sheathed in the floaty fabric. His mind turned to his beloved Catherine. *She had been olive-skinned and deliciously exotic.* He extinguished the thought. *I must not compare Annabelle to Catherine.* He wondered what had prompted these thoughts and hoped they would retreat to whence they came.

Annabelle was always a private person. The spacious house in Mayfair enabled that privacy. In the suite, solitude was more difficult. *I shall wear the gown since it covers nearly all of me. There is no harm in it, I suppose?*

Even though they had spent many years together as friends, she never became over-familiar. They discussed and debated many subjects, but she never gave the slightest hint that there was any more than innocent companionship between them.

"Miss Annabelle, how many firesides have we shared?"

She smiled at the curious but thoughtful question.

"Hundreds, perhaps even thousands, Sam."

The thought of it made her feel warm inside, just as the gentle heat from the fire made her face rosy too.

Within the week, it would be time to say goodbye to Paris.

"Papa," said Shilling, "we haven't seen everything yet."

"You will have something for next time then, won't you," answered Samuel keen to close down the conversation and finish packing.

"But, Papa—"

"No buts, Shilling, it's time to leave. We have responsibilities at home and people to look after."

"But you have foremen, Papa, who can take care of that," challenged a forceful Shilling, flicking her dark hair back, green eyes flashing.

It was one of the rare times that Samuel didn't smile at her. *I fear she is developing a most unattractive air of entitlement. She has been spared a harsh childhood like mine, and now that is beginning to have consequences. It needs nipping in the bud.*

"Shilling, I want you to remember something, and I hope I never have to repeat it. We are responsible for the people who work in my factories. Their toil pays for our excellent standard of living. In return, we are responsible for giving them employment and good wages. To meet that responsibility, we have to work hard to be able to take them under our wing. We will not treat them poorly, as if they are expendable, like Sir Charles Buckingham and his ilk. They are not our slaves. They are real people. We pay them the best rates in the industry and take care of their families. We look to those progressive firms owned by the likes of the Cadbury brothers, the Guinness family and the cotton mill titan Titus

Salt, where loyal workers are looked after, respected and nurtured."

He was growing more serious by the minute.

"One day, like Phoebe Webster, you may have to lead our engineering company, and I want you to understand that without our staff we would be nothing. It pains me to say it, but as a woman, you will need their loyalty to stand any chance of commanding the best from them, in fact, anything from the workers at all. So, I will not tolerate this selfish arrogance from you. You have been privileged, Shilling. You do not understand what it means to be poor. You will work as hard as they do and reciprocate the loyalty they bestow upon us."

He offered an olive branch after one final rebuke.

"Also, I want you to start respecting Miss Wallace. Continue your curriculum with her, and indulge her if you must when she asks you to study topics you find displeasing. When you are eighteen, I will hire a tutor who is proficient in your scientific interests."

Shilling sat down on the sofa without saying a word. Papa did not get fierce often. *What did he mean by 'You do not understand what it means to be poor?' Of course, I know what poor means. I've seen the beggars and the sweeps, haven't I?*

Nevertheless, her father's sermon played on her mind throughout her entire voyage home, and she made a commitment not to disappoint him again.

16

THE SEARCH FOR A SECOND TUTOR

It was now December, 1867, and Shilling, the girl, had become a young woman.

She was lounging comfortably in Samuel's study. He watched his daughter. Her thick dark hair was tied in a knot at the nape of her neck, and her thickly-lashed green eyes were focused on him. He noted that her long lanky arms and legs had filled out. Her body had curves. She had developed breasts and cultivated a small waist. She was becoming more attractive, sensual even. Samuel felt uncomfortable making these observations, and he discarded any further thoughts of his daughter's evolution to womanhood.

He was about to raise the subject of a new machine he had purchased for the foundry, but she spoke before he could mention it.

"Papa, have you chosen a tutor for me yet, now I am eighteen?"

Samuel looked up.

"I think Uncle John may have found someone. His name is Baxter Lee, and he has studied in America and is at the forefront of understanding new engineering developments. He has a good reputation for teaching mathematics and engineering and is also knowledgeable in chemistry and physics. Uncle John and I will meet with him next week for an interview and make him an offer if he is appropriate for the role. He will then decide if he wants the post."

"Well, Papa, it will be a privilege for him to work for a successful industrialist like you. It will feature well on his résumé. I am sure he will agree."

"It hasn't been easy getting his attention, Shilling. I don't need to remind you that you are a woman, and tutors don't often teach these subjects to ladies—"

"Elizabeth the First had five tutors, Papa."

"She was a queen, Shilling. No one would refuse to educate the monarch. For you, however, it is taking a lot more negotiating. I have had to offer him a not insignificant salary to persuade him just to consider the idea."

"Are you serious, Papa? He doesn't want to teach me purely because I am a woman?"

Rather than give her another harsh dose of reality, he humoured his daughter.

"Yes, Shilling, can you believe it? Your grandmother and I ran the farm near Birmingham. If the plough broke and I wasn't there to help, my mother would fix that plough all on her own. Now, this man is telling me that women don't have the aptitude for engineering. He should have met your grandmother."

Samuel gave a knowing smile and a cheerful nod at the memory of his industrious mother.

"Oh, Papa, you are so funny. I hope that Mr Lee is worth all the trouble he is creating for you."

"We will see. Uncle John is impressed, but I will make up my own mind. If we offer the position and he accepts it will take him a month until he can begin teaching. What are you going to do to keep yourself busy while we wait for him?"

Shilling was standing up now and leaning with her hands on the back of Samuel's chair.

"Well, Papa, there may be another reform bill passed in the next few months. Bedford College is well established. Henry Morley at King's College has been fighting for women's education for some years now. I will find a place where I can quietly sit in a corner and listen to all the opinions on the subject. I can also attend talks. The library has anterooms where science and politics are discussed. If I am very quiet, they don't notice a woman in the room."

"Politics? Since when did you develop an interest in politics?"

"Since I was old enough to read your newspaper, Papa," said Shilling with a gleam in her eye. "Oh, and the library has some articles on a Scottish fellow who says he can eradicate infectious bacteria. Lister, I think, is his name? I also read about Martha Coston. She used her chemistry and firework design skills to create coloured communication flares for shipping."

Samuel shook his head and smiled. She never ceased to surprise him.

"Oh Papa, once I have settled into my studies, can you show me the street where I was born and the cemetery where my mother is buried?"

"Yes, of cour—What?"

Out of habit, Samuel had started to agree, then suddenly stopped. It took a few seconds for the gravity to register about her throwaway request.

"I thought it would be a good time to see where you found me, Papa." She replied, in a matter of fact way. "And I want to see where you buried my mother. I am a woman myself now, Papa. There are things I need to know about my origins."

Samuel was speechless. At that moment, he couldn't answer her.

Of all the questions she could have asked him today, he would never have guessed that this would be the one. Shilling had absolute faith that he would consent to the request. She was unaware of his surprise. He managed to keep it well hidden. *It's not just Clare being there, it's the others. How can I ever contemplate going back? There is nothing but heartache there for me.*

Blissfully unaware of his anguish, Shilling kissed him on the cheek:

"I love you, Papa."

"I love you too, my dearest."

17

SO, WHERE DID I COME FROM, PAPA?

When Shilling had left the room, Samuel leaned over his desk and put his head in his hands. He sat like that for an hour. At last, he got up and walked to the door. He opened it roughly and put his head around it, bellowing:

"Socrates, come here now."

It resounded through the house. Socrates was convinced that something terrible was happening. He ran to Samuel's study. He didn't need to knock; the door was wide open.

"Sir! What has happened?" asked his bewildered right-hand man, picking up on the seriousness of the situation.

"Pour us each a drink."

Socrates poured them both a whisky. The drinks cabinet was only used when he had to offer guests refreshment, so he was rightly confused.

"But you don't drink, Sir?"

"Once in a blue moon, I do, Socrates," and with that, he demolished the honey-coloured liquor in a single gulp once more.

He shuddered. *It tastes as bad as the whisky I drank with John the day I announced I intended to marry Catherine.*

"Sit down, Socrates."

"Yes, Sir."

"I want you to have the cab ready at eleven o'clock on Friday morning, please. Shilling wants to go to the street where she was born and visit her mother's grave. She was expecting to go later in the year between her studies, but I think the matter is best addressed as soon as possible."

Samuel said it flatly without any sentiment, despite feeling extremely emotional inside.

Socrates gently enquired:

"Are you alright, Samuel?"

It was probably the first time he, personally, had ever used his master's first name. He knew that Samuel was afraid, that he didn't welcome the memories of the poor blood-soaked Irish girl lying dead in the gutter, nor to contemplate what might have happened had Shilling not been snatched from ragged Maggie Carrott's clutches, the wicked anatomists' supplier. He knew the poor widowed husband didn't want to go back to Catherine's grave shared with his perfect twin sons, nor Clare Byrne's.

"You don't have to do this, Samuel. Perhaps, I can take Shilling and Miss Annabelle?"

"I would never do that, Socrates. What kind of person would I be to burden Miss Annabelle with this? She has her own trauma from the past. God knows if I should even mention this to her. She cannot possibly go there it would devastate her. No, this is a task for me, well us, and us alone, Socrates."

"Sir, I will have the cab ready at eleven sharp on Friday."

"Thank you, dear friend."

"Please tell Shilling in private. Oh, and not a word to Miss Annabelle. Agreed?"

"Right you are, Sir."

"Shilling and I need to take this important journey together—the two of us as father and daughter."

The crisp wintery morning was spectacular. The sun shone bright, and the sky was a clear azure blue. Samuel assisted Shilling into the cab and then followed her inside. He didn't feel like speaking. He couldn't anyway; he was terrified. If he spoke one word, his trembling voice would have given him away.

Shilling was cheerful but aware of the melancholy suffocating her father. They were too close for her not to sense his troubled mind, no matter how hard he tried to conceal it. She was sensitive enough to keep quiet for once and let him be with his thoughts.

"Wapping, Sir?" asked Socrates.

"Yes, please."

"Did he say Wapping, Papa?" asked Shilling, a frown appearing on her beautifully smooth face.

"Yes," answered Samuel.

"But Papa isn't is a hazardous area, full of rogues, ruffians, knaves and—"

"Yes, it is." he interrupted briskly.

Samuel had no desire to discuss it further, and the next part of the journey continued in silence.

18

THE RETURN TO WAPPING

The expedition was exciting for someone like Shilling who had never done it before. They began their route, passing beautiful mansions and parks where people were cheerfully strolling or riding. As they drove toward Wapping, the scenery out of the carriage window began to change. The streets narrowed. What few open spaces there were looked much smaller, and were sparsely populated with a handful of trees. The people were different too. They looked tired, battle-weary, she supposed. Their dress was neat but not smart.

When almost at their final destination, the most noticeable change was the abundance of ragged little children playing in the dirty streets. *This could have been my life?* Their parents were yelling at them in a vernacular that Shilling could not understand. It sounded like another language. Samuel understood every word but was unable to raise his spirits enough to translate.

For the last few hundred feet, there were no more pavements. Human life was now dirty and unkempt. Drunken beggars littered the streets and the children ran wild rather than played. The stench of the overflowing middens was unbearable. Shilling put her handkerchief over her mouth after giving up trying to hold her breath.

When the cab occasionally had to stop, strange women would stand and yell comments by the window. Samuel pulled down the blind. Thankfully, Shilling wasn't aware of the nature of their suggestions. Young dockers ran about the area, hard at work. Sailors, worse for wear, stumbled out of pubs.

The cab turned into a very narrow side street. Samuel had never come back here, and after eighteen years, nothing had changed. The pavement had huge potholes in it. Horse dung littered the space, and raw sewage ran along the gutters. Bazelgette's planned eighty-two miles of super sewer were yet to reach Wapping.

Socrates stopped the cab. Samuel was grateful that the street was quiet, unlike a lot of the thoroughfares through the dockland area.

"Why are we stopping, Papa?" asked Shilling nervously, feeling extremely unsettled by their current surroundings.

"This is the spot. We need to alight now."

"Here—Papa?"

Socrates opened the cab door. Samuel stepped out and assisted Shilling onto the road. Shilling's beauty was out of place in this filthiest of streets. Her face was solemn. All the jollity of the coming festive season was snuffed out. She did her best to stop her skirt dragging along the foetid floor.

Samuel was very quiet. Socrates made his way to his side. He whispered a suggestion so softly that Shilling would not hear him.

"Sir, let us get the task over with. I will go ahead, just follow me. It will be over in a flash, you'll see."

Samuel barely nodded, despite Socrates calm conviction that everything would be alright. Also, in an attempt to be supportive, Shilling took her father's arm in her hand at the elbow. He covered her hand protectively.

The drive had taken approximately an hour. The sun was higher still in the sky. Brightly illuminating the street, its harsh light was unforgiving. There were no shadows, and the sheer horror of the scene around them was so blatant and shocking that Shilling fell behind her father, allowing him to go one pace ahead of her.

The stench caught in her throat. It was the stench of excrement, decay, disease and death. It was crawling all over her, down her gullet and up her nose with every breath that she took, and she wanted to scrub herself clean but couldn't. *How can a place like this even exist?*

Socrates found the steps that he had climbed back in that dark December day in 1849, this time unimpeded by the onlookers. He felt it would help him pinpoint the exact location. He took a brief look then returned to the street and stopped about twenty yards further on. He didn't look around. He didn't need to. The memory of the events he witnessed all those years ago was still so fresh in his mind it could have been yesterday.

Socrates made reassuring eye contact with Samuel, and seemed to will him forward one step at a time. Shilling followed him. On reaching Socrates, they all stood motionless.

"This is where you were born," said Samuel flatly.

He could do no more than that. His mouth was dry. Horrible, distressing memories kept flashing through his mind, and he was struggling to put the pictures into the correct sequence.

Shilling looked around her.

"Here? Not in a bed—or even—a building?
Straight on these grimy cobbles?" She asked.

With her spirit crushed by the brutal reality of her repulsive entrance to the world, all the more confusing with her current privileged existence, she barely took the situation in. She did not know what she expected, but she was sure she hadn't supposed a hellish nightmare of a place like this. She felt a spiralling mishmash of feelings, anger, relief, disappointment, gratitude and shame.

"Really? Here? But how? Why?" she demanded trying to make sense of it. Feeling lost and desperate to be heard, Shilling's voice was louder than usual, bordering on shrill.

Still a paralysed Samuel said nothing.

"Here, Papa? Answer me! Here? Is this where I was born? Is this what I actually am?"

Now her voice was penetrating. Samuel could still not bring himself to speak. Shilling was furious. *This is a time for truth, not silence, Papa.*

Socrates stepped forward in an attempt to calm the situation down. She was wild, virtually hysterical and began to sob until her body could no longer stand without swaying dangerously. She didn't care anymore that her skirt was dragging along the foul ground.

"Yes, here, Miss. Your mother struggled off the ship from Ireland when it docked. We found a ticket with her name on it in a small bag she had with her. She was weakened by the famine and only made it this far from the quayside. I believe she was trying to get to a friend or relative's house but never made it. That's all I know. I'm sorry."

Socrates tried to calm her down. She fought and struggled as he tried to put his arm around her in case she collapsed with shock. She wanted to run far away from the awful truth of her origin. He held her until she stopped fighting. She was still visibly upset but also quiet now. He took her back to the cab and helped her up the steps and did his best to clean the dirt off the hem of her skirt.

She looked through the open door. Her father was standing motionless in the same spot with his back to her. Socrates was now next to him, speaking quietly.

"Sir, this is not a place of death anymore. This is a place of hope. This is where you saved Shilling's life, and this is where you exchanged death for love, dark for light, sadness for hope. You never have to return here again. Please come to the cab and take care of your daughter, she needs you now more than ever."

Socrates was firm, and in a strange reversal of the chain of command, Samuel complied.

"Yes. Thank you, my good fellow. You're right," he said with gratitude as they returned to the carriage.

Socrates softly closed Shilling's door and opened the one on his master's side, and with a nod, beckoned him to walk towards him.

He climbed into the cab and sat next to Shilling. He gently took her trembling hand in his, and together they rode along solemnly to their next location on their unpleasant, eye-opening tour. There would be more horror to come before they would return, with renewed gratitude, to their safe haven in Mayfair.

She didn't say a word when they arrived at Highgate cemetery. Shilling and Samuel walked past the trees, past the tombs and vaults. At last, they stopped at a large plot surrounded by decorative cast-iron railings which were rusting from years of neglect. It was overgrown with creepers and wildflowers. There were two inscriptions on the large, impressive carved stone sarcophagus, one at each end.

The first one she saw read:

Clare Byrne
The Beautiful Mother of Shilling
Died December 1849

The second inscription read:

In loving memory of
Catherine Hudson
Luke Hudson & Peter Hudson
wife and children of
Samuel Hudson
1844

The day was taking an unusual turn. Shilling was getting a gritty glimpse of her father's past. She was ashamed that it had taken this experience for her to realise what he had done for her. She moved closer to him.

"Papa, you never told me."

"It was a long time ago, Shilling."

"And Socrates, you never told me, either," she said, feeling curiously betrayed yet still understanding why they might want to spare her from the truth.

It was not an accusatory comment but instead borne out of nothing more than an intense inquisitiveness. It was said with the most profound respect.

"Shilling, I never ever wanted you to feel that you were some sort of—replacement," said Samuel gently.

She looked bitterly sad at the suggestion.

"Miss Shilling, before your father took the money out of his pocket to pay for you, he told the wretch to give him 'his child'. In his mind, you were his child from the moment he saw you. Thanks to him, you are not in the gutter today, Shilling. You have been blessed with everything you need to be a fine woman. Perhaps one day, you will be able to return the favour to someone who also needs support. To reiterate what he told you in Paris, let today remind you of how far you have come, and how far down you could have sunk into poverty, were it not for your father's generosity lifting you up."

The gravity of the situation and her harsh surroundings helped her finally understand her father's words back then. *No, I haven't experienced true poverty, and I do take things for granted. For all my education, I can be terribly imbecilic at times.*

Samuel nodded in agreement on hearing Socrates's words. Her father had forgotten the lecture he'd given her in France four years ago about her ugly sense of entitlement, but now it was evident in his mind again. *It must have had an impact upon her. I hope she continues to remember.*

"Papa, will you tell me about Catherine and the two boys?" asked Shilling.

"No, it is in the past now. You can discuss it with Socrates if you wish, but I do not want to talk about it anymore."

"Was it terrible, Papa?" she asked earnestly.

"Yes, it was terrible, but time has moved on, and it is not something for you to be concerned about."

"I am sorry, Papa. I wish I could make it better for you."

"You did make it better, Shilling, from the day I took you home. You brought me joy after years of grief."

She hugged him, then kissed him on the cheek:

"I love you so much, Papa."

She smiled at him. She had never given a thought to the idea that her father had a life before she arrived. She was very serious as she began walking back to the cab. In one day, her outlook was painfully and swiftly transformed from a carefree child to a worldly-wise adult.

"Sir, would you like to be alone for a while?"

"No thank you, Socrates. I'd like to go straight home."

A drained and grief-stricken Samuel wanted to say, *'straight home to Miss Annabelle,'* but thought it best not to. It seemed far too inappropriate, even under the extreme circumstances.

19

THANK GOD THAT IS OVER

In the twilight, Samuel lay on the bed in his room. There was a tranquillity to this time of the day, and he always enjoyed watching the sky fade to black until the heavens were pitch dark and the stars twinkled. He thought about the day's events.

Thank God that is over. Shilling will be fine. She is resilient. And thank God for Socrates, I could not have got through the day without the man. I am so lucky to have someone so loyal at my side.

As he lay there, a loneliness overcame him. He knew that he was emotionally exhausted and it exacerbated his feeling of being isolated. He meant to close his eyes for just a short while. Instead, he fell asleep fully clothed.

Samuel was awoken by a soft knock on the door and Socrates entered.

"Sir, may I come in? Can I bring your dinner to you?"

"What is the time?" asked Samuel while he shed his jacket and waistcoat, ripped off his tie and undid his top button.

"Eleven o'clock in the evening, Sir."

Samuel's head was fuzzy, and he was struggling to wake up.

"That late. Oh my. Thank you for thinking of me. May I please have tea and something light to eat. Tell cook not to go to the trouble of making a hot meal."

"Yes, Sir. Of course. I'll have her see to it."

"And is Miss Annabelle still awake?" he enquired.

"Yes, Sir, I believe she is. There is still a light on in her room."

Samuel climbed the stairs to the third floor. He passed Shilling's room—it was in darkness. He was glad she was able to get some rest. He went on up to Miss Annabelle's bedroom. There was a sliver of light under the door. For eighteen years Samuel had never been into her room. She had always come to see him in the schoolroom or study.

He knocked and asked if he may enter. Politely, she opened the door.

Her room was more like a suite than a roof-top garret usually reserved for governesses or servants. She had a large comfortable sofa in front of a small marble fire-place. At the window, there was a petite regency dining room table with two chairs. On the wall opposite was a French writing desk, inlaid with beautiful gold patterns, with a matching seat. The bed was a half-tester, draped with soft fabrics. He decided the room would be light and feminine in the day. The walls were covered in a pale silk damask and hanging from the picture rails were the most exquisite oil paintings that Samuel had ever seen. Where she had run out of space to hang them, she simply leaned them against the walls.

Samuel stood with his hands in his pockets, pretending to examine the art. He was far more aware that she was wearing the same French dressing gown she had worn in Paris.

"These paintings are gorgeous, Miss Annabelle. You have the most excellent taste."

"I invested in them, Samuel. They are valuable enough to buy me a small home one day."

The thought of Annabelle leaving had never really crossed his mind. He always assumed she would be there to look after Shilling. However, it suddenly dawned upon him that his daughter was now an adult living under his roof and wouldn't need caring for much longer. *That means she might soon leave! After all the thoughts today of death and life being over in the blink of an eye—things you knew already— what have you been doing all these years, Samuel? Asleep on the job, it seems. Remember, time waits for no man.*

He snapped his brain back to the room.

"Shilling and I often go to galleries, and I began to research art as an investment."

"So, you bought them?"

"Well, I didn't steal them, Samuel! You pay me a comfortable wage, and I have no expenses. The artworks gain value, so it made sense to buy some."

He was grateful for her levity. It cheered him up.

"I should put you in charge of my investments."

He gave a deep laugh, although strangely, he still felt deeply uncomfortable in the room. It was her private space. *And I keep having these intrusive romantic thoughts.*

"Um, Socrates has made me tea and something light to eat, would you care to join me?"

"Yes, of course." she smiled.

It was socially unbecoming for Annabelle to meet in Samuel's bedroom, but out of expediency, she had done so on several occasions before that night to tend to Shilling when she had been ill and wanted to be with her father. Samuel was a law unto himself, and to him, societal norms caused complications in his busy existence. That evening, in his room, she was quite comfortable sitting on the buttoned-leather couch, discussing the poignant day's events.

He stood at the tea trolley, piled high with enough sandwiches to feed a small army, with his sleeves rolled, top button undone and shirttails hanging out in his usual relaxed style. He poured her a cup of tea and handed it to her. Annabelle curled up in the corner of the couch to make room for him. Samuel chose to sit on the floor, his back resting on the padded seat, leaving the space next to her empty. Samuel gazed into the fire. He knew he had to confide in her, knowing he was safe in her presence. Feeling a little less alone, he let down his guard and his oppressive, dark thoughts of the day tumbled out.

"I took Shilling to Wapping and Highgate cemetery today."

"Why on earth would you do that, Sam?"

"Shilling was curious. Now she is eighteen, she wanted to see that awful street that she was born in. It was terrible. It had been her idea all along, not mine I can assure you. She looked so hurt. I don't know how I would have got through it without Socrates. Then, we took her to where her mother is buried. She insisted on seeing the grave.

"—graves", he corrected. "She has a right to know more about where she came from, I suppose, so how could I refuse?"

"Oh, Sam, I would have come with you, supported you."

"I couldn't do that to you, Annabelle. I know how much it hurt you losing little baby Sarah."

"I made peace with my loss many years ago, Samuel. Don't you worry about me anymore."

She was silent for a while, then spoke softly.

"Sam, why were you so traumatised at going back to Wapping. I can understand Shilling, but why you? You knew where you were going."

"Annabelle, as I stood there, in my mind's eye, I saw Shilling's mother lying in a filthy gutter. She was such a beautiful young girl. She was so broken. Her dress was hitched up, and she was lying in a huge pool of black, sticky blood. I looked at her that day, and all that I could see was Catherine."

"But Catherine was sick and died with the fever, Samuel. She died at home. You said the doctor did all he could, remember?"

"I'm sorry, Annabelle, but that was a little white lie I told you to spare your feelings. No one in this house will talk about the awful business that day because they are loyal to me. It wasn't the sickness that took her, she died giving birth. The babies were laying incorrectly, breeched, the doctor said. They were twin boys, both stillborn."

Annabelle looked at him with a mix of shock and sympathy as he continued.

"It was terrible. Catherine was so vibrant. I couldn't accept that she was dead. It sounds wicked, but I would have sacrificed those two babies for her. I promise you, Annabelle, if I knew it would kill her, I would have gouged them from her at the start."

"Samuel, I didn't realise—" Her face was aghast. After that, she was lost for words for a while.

Samuel didn't take his eyes off the fire. He couldn't reply. *Now, I've said it. Now she knows.* Despite the gravity of his revelations, at that moment he felt nothing, except perhaps unburdened.

She moved off the sofa and sat next to him on the floor. She put his arm across his chest and her hand over his breaking heart to comfort him. He did not respond.

"Sam," she said gently. "Look at me."

Nothing—.

Out of frustration, she climbed on his legs and sat astride his thighs. She turned his face towards her and looked into his eyes.

"Look at me. Sam, look at me!" she insisted.

He gazed at her sadly and whispered:

"No one should ever have to feel this pain."

She beheld the handsome man before her with the utmost compassion and understanding. He pulled her towards him as she kneeled. *Is now the time?* She lay her torso on his chest. Her ear was close to his mouth, and she felt his rhythmic breathing.

"You do know that I love you, Annabelle?" he murmured.

"Yes, I do. I have for years, Sam," she answered.

"Will you—stay with me tonight?" he asked tentatively as he brushed his hand gently across her forehead, past her cheek and down through her hair.

"Yes." was her reply.

20

TRUSTING ONE'S GUT INSTINCTS

Samuel employed Shilling's tutor, Baxter Lee, against his better judgement. John Green had to spend quite a few hours convincing him that he was making the correct decision.

"Samuel, you don't have to like the man, but you must admit that he is an expert in the field of mathematics and science. Why are you so reluctant to appoint him?"

"John, I agree that his skills are top class, but it is his character that makes me doubt him."

John laughed.

"What do you know about character, Sam, you're a simple farm boy at heart."

"Indeed, I am. And may I remind you, farm boys are the most qualified to see a wolf in sheep's clothing," scowled Samuel in response.

"Has Mr Lee offended you?"

"No, he has not bloody offended me. Perhaps that's exactly the problem. He is too agreeable."

Samuel chuckled, showing John that it was a fatherly concern and not an academic one at the heart of his misgivings.

"On a more serious note, Samuel, you can always end his contract if you are unhappy, but Shilling will not respect someone with lesser qualification. The other thing is, of course, she's 'a woman'. How many tutors of this calibre want to teach a female student? Not very many is the answer you are looking for."

Samuel knew that it was true. John had gone to a lot of trouble to procure Mr Lee's services, and yes, he was the best tutor he had interviewed. It was just that the man was so different to all the academics Samuel had met before. They were usually old and crusty, smelling of snuff, dusk, chalk and encyclopaedias. The dashing Baxter Lee was anything but.

John Green was invited for dinner, and Shilling found him waiting in the parlour. It was about six months since John last saw her, and he was startled by how much she had matured in a short while.

Shilling was wearing a burgundy dress without any fussy frills or lace. The skirt wasn't as full as was fashionable, but she hated all the paraphernalia that came with wearing the latest ladies' fashions, it felt less like clothing and more like a moveable installation.

Her long hair was still kept off her face by the beautiful small silver hair comb in the shape of a butterfly her father had made for her. The sleeves of the dress were just off the shoulder, exposing her flawless, creamy white skin.

Around her neck, she wore a large emerald pendant, the size of a penny, on a gold chain. Samuel had given her the necklace for her eighteenth birthday, and she loved it. The colour of the emerald matched the shade of her eyes. Her smile was wide.

Shilling wasn't overly tall for a woman, but she had a strong presence that filled the room, making her seem bigger than she was. Her body had perfect proportions with sensuous curves that made up her full bosom and petite waistline.

John caught himself wondering about what lay beneath the dress but corrected himself when he realised how disloyal he was to his good friend Samuel.

"Oh hello, Uncle John, I am so sorry you are waiting alone. Where is Papa?"

"Good evening, Shilling. You look beautiful tonight. I believe your father has Mr Lee in his study. They are finalising his contract of employment."

"That is wonderful news, thank you for assisting Papa with choosing a tutor for me. He said you went to a lot of trouble to convince Mr Lee to work with me."

"It's a pleasure, Shilling. Ah! Here comes your father."

Samuel came striding into the parlour. He was still a handsome man, and he was ageing well. His hair was greying a little at the temples, but his body was still athletic, and his face only had fine wrinkles at the eyes and corners of his mouth. He could still carry off the look of boyish charm, and over the past few days seemed to have regained the sparkle in his eye.

Baxter Lee followed Samuel into the room.

"Hello, John, Shilling. Let me introduce you, please."

His daughter stepped forward boldly.

"Shilling, this is Mr Baxter Lee, your new tutor. Mr Lee, this is Miss Hudson, my daughter."

Baxter Lee also took a step forward, and Shilling shook his hand confidently.

"How do you do, Mr Lee. Please call me Shilling, everyone else does."

She gave him her best dazzling smile. Baxter Lee smiled too, but his was disingenuous. He noted her simple but elegant style and the emerald at her throat. *Another wealthy, pretty, spoilt brat, I see. This will be no different to all my other tedious tutoring posts. If it weren't for the extra money for teaching a woman—*. He gazed down at her and hoped that she had some form of intelligence, or the next few years would be terribly dull.

Annabelle didn't just arrive, she positively floated into the room. The secret of Annabelle's beauty lay in her serenity. The gentle smile and soft eyes communicated a calm soul. Annabelle was nearly forty now but looked ten years younger.

She was wearing a white lace dress, and her hair was plaited into a loose knot behind her head. She was very fair, and her blue eyes were sparkling.

John Green was always particularly fond of her, and he was delighted to see her looking so well. He decided to do the next introduction.

> "Good evening, Miss Annabelle. This is Mr Baxter Lee, Shilling's new tutor. Annabelle has been instrumental in raising Mr Hudson's daughter."

Annabelle shook his hand and smiled, then took a glass of sherry and sat down.

She watched Mr Lee. He was neither as distinguished or as handsome as Samuel but was a similar height. Physically, he defied the traditional appearance of an intellectual, looking a little more athletic and bohemian than academic and bookish.

He had his dark hair in a closely cropped style. Rather curiously for a new employee, he had half a day's stubble that cast a shadow on his face. *So, that's where his bohemian demeanour comes from, I suppose.* In his mid-twenties, he was a good-looking man and gave no impression of still being a boy.

Socrates announced that dinner was served and the small party moved toward the dining room.

The table was prepared for five people. Samuel, Miss Annabelle, and Shilling at one end, Baxter Lee and John at the other. The seat opposite Samuel, at the far end of the table, remained unoccupied.

Shilling opened the conversation.

"Mr Lee, Papa says that you have been to America. That must have been a wonderful experience."

"Yes. The Americans have a thriving scientific community."

"Which university were you associated with?"

"I read for my degree at the respected Massachusetts Institute of Technology. It is a very new concept, a university dedicated entirely to the sciences, but in my opinion, an excellent approach."

"That is very interesting. I am in correspondence with Mr William Barton Rogers."

Baxter's eyes widened just a little.

"How were you introduced? He is the founder of the university?"

"I wrote a letter asking for information on the developments into electromagnetic energy. I understood that there was some leading research being undertaken at the time."

"And he replied to a woman?" he asked in a puzzled tone.

"Yes, Mr Lee. He did. Because I pretended to be a man."

He smiled at her resourcefulness. *Perhaps this might not be as bad a tenure as I first anticipated.*

"Yes, I am surprised that you chose engineering as a profession. Most women won't get their hands dirty."

"Perhaps that is an accurate observation of the upper classes, Mr Lee, but we Hudson's come from a long line of farmers and my grandmother could fix a plough."

Samuel lifted his hand to his face to stifle a smile. *That's my girl, nothing is going to stop her.*

After the meal, Samuel and Socrates retreated briefly to Samuel's study.

"Socrates, will you please arrange Mr Lee's accommodation?"

"Yes, Sir. May I place him on the second floor?"

"No. It will be the basement or the stables," answered Samuel.

"Yes, Sir, I will arrange it."

Samuel looked at him in amusement, wondering if Socrates would explain to Baxter that he would need to lie on some hay next to the horses, should he choose the stables option, but his trusty assistant was too intelligent to rise to the bait.

"Sir, there is a small flat above the stables and the coach house. I believe it is suitable for our purposes. I will arrange to furnish it and open the chimney up. It has two rooms and a small range for cooking. However, I believe it is planned he will eat in the dining room with the family every night?"

"What gave you that idea? No, Socrates, he will only eat with us when he is invited to. His dinner can be served either in the kitchen here or delivered to his quarters, whichever he prefers."

"Yes, Sir."

The former schoolroom that had been the domain of Miss Wallace was to be upgraded to a laboratory using some technical specifications stipulated by Mr Lee.

Baxter had been particular about the equipment he wanted to secure. Some specialist items had to be imported from America and France. He had it brought with him on his arrival.

"When do your classes commence, Mr Lee?"

"Our lectures will begin tomorrow at nine o'clock, Sir."

"I make no bones about it—besides you will discover for yourself soon enough—my inquisitive daughter is quite a challenge. I don't care if you have a problem with her personality— make sure that you cope with it. Your task is to mentor her until she achieves that university degree. Oh, and you may find she'll accomplish it sooner than you believe her capable of."

Baxter drew up a rigorous schedule for Shilling to adhere to. He was testing her boundaries and deliberately demanding more from her than he would have if she was a man. *Let's see if she is as good as she thinks she is.*

He wanted her in the laboratory bright and early at seven o'clock sharp each day. They would eat breakfast at nine, then study theory. Lunch would be at noon and afternoons would be dedicated to experiments, exhibitions or talks at the university.

It was a challenge getting Shilling to accept this strictly imposed timetable. Further, the cultural obstacles to be overcome outside the household were considerable too. With reluctance, Samuel enabled his daughter to attend by paying many an academic to turn a blind eye to a young woman in their lecture hall. In fact, he had gone so far as to suggest that she dress as a man, but Baxter preferred the subtle arts of bribery to male impersonation.

The first day ended at five o'clock. It gave Shilling some time to herself after her lessons and before dining.

Two hours before the family evening meal, a furtive Samuel gave a single quiet tap on Annabelle's door. These days he no longer felt uncomfortable visiting her quarters, but he wasn't ready for the rest of the household to be aware of their deepening romance just yet. She opened the door and invited him in with that gentle smile that made him feel that he was the only man in the universe. With the door latch clicking closed behind them, he grabbed her around the waist, pulled her toward him and kissed her.

"I missed you, Miss Annabelle." He said as he nuzzled against her neck.

She brushed her cheek softly against his hair to show the feeling was mutual. He lifted his head and asked:

"Do we need to discuss anything important tonight?"

"No. I believe the first day's lessons were a success. I asked both Shilling and Mr Lee privately. I don't think there was any other business on which to confer."

Samuel teased himself away from her and sat on the bed, then lay down, his fingers brushing against the soft canopy drapes as he waited expectantly.

"Well, I have something very important to discuss with you. I need your opinion. Please come here if you will."

She slowly paced over to him, then lay by his side, curious about the important matter that was playing on his mind.

"Miss Annabelle, I have a question," he said. His hands were now moving up and down her body. *What can this question be?* He kissed her hands and her face and finally her mouth. As he broke away, he said:

"Annabelle, marry me. Ahem—excuse my manners. I mean, will you marry me?"

She smiled. This confident, commanding man was fumbling over his presumably well-rehearsed proclamation. Tantalisingly, perhaps annoyingly, she didn't answer immediately. Samuel decided to fill the silence with words, any words, as it made the wait more bearable.

"You see, we have been alone—you and I both, for many years. We have lived here together almost as man and wife since 1849. Therefore—.

Oh, damn it, Annabelle, I love you, I want to marry you. Please, say you will be my wife? You make me happy beyond belief, and you are beautiful, inside and out."

She smiled that tender, warm smile he adored. It reached her eyes as they wrinkled at the corners, then it reached his heart.

"Stop, Sam, Stop! Yes, I will marry you."

The nervous chatter stopped as he kissed her deeply and passionately. Then, he stood up and fumbled around in his jacket pocket. In his hand was a ring. It was a square aquamarine surrounded by diamonds set in white gold. He slipped it onto her finger, and it fitted perfectly.

"Oh Sam, is this for me?"

Annabelle was overwhelmed. For years she had always remained so humble, keeping a polite distance, and now their romance was gathering speed. The thought of this loyal, charming man giving her such a luxurious, expensive ring and wanting to marry her was a lot to take in. *We've come a long way since that fateful night in Wapping.*

"What about Shilling?" asked Annabelle.

"This time, it's about you Annabelle; not Shilling."

He kissed her again and didn't stop for a long time.

21

WHO DID I SEE THIS MORNING

For the past couple of nights after the proposal, Samuel woke up early at six-thirty so he could leave Annabelle's room undetected. Today was no exception. She was sleeping peacefully next to him. He looked at her serene face. Her hand lay on the pillow. He saw the sparkling ring which she only wore in secret in bed for the time being and smiled proudly. *She is beautiful. And she wants to be mine. How lucky a man am I?*

Her shoulders were uncovered, and he ran his hand over her alluring body. *If I don't move now, I will stay here all day, and that simply won't do.*

Reluctantly, Samuel climbed out of bed and dressed. He opened the door and stealthily made his way downstairs to his room on the first floor, a little later than planned, at ten to seven. He found it so hard to leave Annabelle.

Shilling brought him joy, but the love he felt for his child was parental and what he felt for his lover was entirely different. It was fleshy, tempting, sensual and magical. *How I long for her already*. His hand slid down the smooth bannister as he tiptoed as quiet as a mouse. He opened the door to his bedroom and smiled on seeing the cushions under his bedclothes meant to look like his sleeping body if there were any unexpected visitors. Now, he was far too excited to sleep. It was time to see what the dawn of a new day would bring.

Every evening at seven-thirty, it became routine for Socrates to deliver a hot meal to Baxter's apartment. Baxter tried his utmost to be friendly, but Socrates was particular about his company, and the young tutor still had to prove himself.

Routinely, he would knock on Mr Lee's door with his toe, his two hands carefully carrying a tray of food, beautifully served on a heated plate, and brought under a hot silver dome to keep it warm.

Baxter felt a little isolated at not being included at the family meal every night and would try to entice Socrates to gossip. This evening was no exception, especially as Mr Lee had some exciting news to share.

Seeing him make his way to his lodgings through a small window, regular as clockwork, Baxter decided to be helpful and opened the door.

"Good evening, Mr Lee."

"Good evening, Socrates. My, that smells delicious. Thank you for bringing it to me."

"Right you are," he replied, swiftly setting the tray down, aiming to get back to the main building as quickly as he could.

A determined Baxter decided to spark up a longer conversation. If he could get Socrates on side, he was a step nearer to dining in the main house and ingratiating himself with Samuel—and his fat wallet. Before his arrival, Mr Lee had poured out two glasses of brandy, hoping it would extend their encounter.

"Shilling did very well in her studies today," he said as he tried to hand a glass to Socrates, who deftly avoided accepting it.

"That is good news," was the predictable and perfunctory reply.

Socrates turned to go, then was forced to stop to answer a question.

"Tell me, is Mr Hudson available?" pushed Baxter, raising his voice a little.

"No, I am afraid not Mr Lee. He is busy this evening."

"And Miss Annabelle?"

"No, Mr Lee, the family is dining a little earlier this evening, and then they have plans."

"What plans?"

"The theatre, I believe."

He was becoming frustrated with Socrates's unhelpful answers. Swirling his brandy around his glass, he watched Socrates prepare to leave. He downed both drinks.

Who does he think he is? Is it me, or does everyone in this close-knit household insist on avoiding me like the plague? Look at him, he can't get out of here quick enough.

"Will there be anything else, Mr Lee?"

"Yes, as a matter of fact, there is."

A vindictive Baxter Lee decided now was the time to unleash his bombshell of news.

"Did you know that Mr Hudson and Miss Annabelle's spent last night in bed together."

Socrates dismissed the suggestion.

"I doubt that very much, Sir. Good evening, Mr Lee."

As he collected his tea towel, he noticed on the tray all the cutlery setting had slid out of position in transit, and the perfectionist in him stopped for a moment to align it properly. It was then that Baxter leaned over and whispered his poisonous revelation under his breath.

"I am not a liar. Your precious master has a live-in whore. I saw him stealthily making his way downstairs as I finished preparing the laboratory and went to wake Shilling for her lessons just before seven. He darted back to his room, foolishly thinking he had got away with his secret night of—"

Socrates spun around quicker than a whirligig. With a fist as mighty as a hammer, he hit Baxter square on the nose. Stunned and bloodied, his nemesis tumbled over his desk. The tray and the carefully prepared food lay on the floor amidst the broken crockery.

Socrates leaned forward, grabbed Baxter by the throat and put him firmly in his place.

"You seem to have forgotten your manners, Mr Lee. I am in charge of the running of this home. Let me explain the house rules. You are not allowed on the second floor. You do not wake up Shilling, is that clear. And if I hear a word of gossip related to Mr Hudson, you will leave this house in an undertaker's basket. Is that understood, Mr Lee?"

The dazed tutor refused to—or couldn't—acknowledge Socrates's request, making him even less tolerant.

"Do you understand me, Mr Lee?" asked Socrates a second time, digging his fingers even further behind his foe's windpipe till the man could barely breathe.

"Yes. I understand, Sir. I do!" rasped Baxter.

With that, Socrates let go of his vice-like grip, slipped out and made his way back to the main house. A baffled cook bumped into him outside in the courtyard.

"I heard quite a commotion from Mr Lee's lodgings just then. It sounded like a lot of crashing and banging about. What happened?"

"I was a clumsy, old butterfingered fool. I dropped the tray," explained Socrates, who preferred to tell a lie for once rather than reveal Baxter's bombshell about Samuel.

Whether this secret liaison is true or not, it is none of my business. And if their actions bring two loyal companions joy, then that is all that matters.

"Shall I dish up another plate for Mr Lee, then?" asked cook kindly.

"No, thank you," replied Socrates. "Apparently, Mr Lee feels a little out of sorts and says he has lost his appetite this evening."

22

THE ANNOUNCEMENT
OVER DINNER

A few days after the fight, Samuel invited John Green and Baxter Lee to dine with the family, the dress code, formal, the time, seven for seven-fifteen.

Cook was asked to prepare an elaborate dinner. Socrates was requested to bring up some champagne from the cellar. Lizzy was told the festivities were to require their most elegant sets of linen, silverware and crystal.

The dining table was decorated with small vases of orchids, and there were large urns of roses arranged around the buffet. Socrates placed snow-white candles in tall silver candelabras. The room sparkled with elegant charm.

Shilling was to join John Green and Baxter in the parlour. There was no sign of Samuel or Annabelle.

Baxter was looking a bit worse for wear with a dark bruise under one eye.

"Whatever happened to you?" asked John with concern.

"Well, I walked into a door. New lodgings— wandering in the unfamiliar gloom at night— I tripped—You know how it is."

He smiled awkwardly as he caught Socrates notice his fibbing. He added mischievously:

"If you need anything from the doctor, please feel free to ask me to arrange it, Mr Lee."

"Thank you, but it is already much better."

"Does anybody know why we have been summoned to this small black-tie event?" asked Shilling. She looked lovely in a modest black and gold dress.

"If I know your father, he has probably acquired another business," laughed John. "I must confess, I haven't been a part of this secret, Shilling."

"Neither have I, Uncle John."

"Ah, here is the man at last," he said, smiling fondly at Samuel. *He's the son I never had.*

"Where is Miss Annabelle?" asked Shilling.

"She will be here presently," said Samuel, with a broad smile.

Promptly at seven-fifteen, Annabelle entered the room. She was wearing the most gorgeous dress. It was silver-grey and embroidered with pink, green and blue flowers. The bodice was tight-fitting, and the sleeves were off the shoulder. Tiny beads sparkled every time she moved, and her hair was twisted into an elegant French knot. She wore no jewellery around her neck. But on her third finger of the left hand was the most beautiful ring that Shilling had ever seen.

"Papa, I think you have been keeping a secret from us?" said Shilling delightedly, looking at the ring and then her beaming father.

"We have. It is true. Annabelle and I have been the best of friends for eighteen years now," said Samuel becoming more serious with each word. "I have realised that I don't want to have a future without her by my side. So, I have asked her to marry me, and she has said yes."

Samuel paused, he was waiting for a volley of questions, but there were none. For the household, the only surprise was that it had taken them so long to be betrothed. There were only the heartiest congratulations. Annabelle was radiant, and Samuel couldn't take his eyes off her.

Socrates smirked as crafty Mr Lee had seen the wind taken out of his treacherous sails. *Good. Everyone knows they are a couple now, so there will be no need for any more tactless bombshells from you, Sonny Jim.*

23

THE EMERALD NECKLACE

It was three-thirty on a Wednesday afternoon. Shilling was in Baxter's bed. The only thing she was wearing was the emerald pendant her father had given her. Baxter was lying next to her fully clothed. He was reading to her from the American Journal of Science. She was utterly absorbed in the subject, but Baxter, on the other hand, was finding it remarkably difficult to focus.

"Please put on your clothes, Shilling, you are distracting me."

Shilling was lying in the crook of his arm with one leg draped over him. Her hair was now waist length, and it flowed across the pillow like waves of silk. He was stroking her nakedness with one hand, and the other was left holding the journal.

"Baxter—Papa and Annabelle are in Birmingham; they will not return for a week. Socrates is with them, and I have outsmarted Lizzy. She believes that I have a frightful headache, and I am resting."

He sighed.

"You have had a lot of headaches lately Shilling, someone is bound to become suspicious."

"Baxter, may I remind you, in a short while I will have my degree and I will be twenty-one, and able to support myself. Papa says as soon as I am self-sufficient, I may manage my life as I wish, and I intend to do that," she said with her characteristic determination.

Her tone made sure Baxter had no doubt about that.

"What does that have to do with dressing?" he asked her.

"It means that I may be naked with whomever I wish and nobody can complain about it."

Baxter cupped her bosom and grinned.

"Well, I, for one, am thrilled that your Papa raised you with such bohemian principles. Now, why don't you take off my clothes and show me how liberal you can be—"

Shilling began to undress him slowly at first, then with a quickening pace as their passions rose.

24

A DIFFERENT SORT OF EDUCATION

By all accounts, Shilling was the most brilliant student that Baxter had ever taught. Not only did she enjoy her subjects as an intellectual, but she was passionate about knowledge, and she continuously challenged everyone and everything with her intellect. Her attitude was that if she did not know everything, she knew nothing.

At the outset of the affair, her submission did not distress him. It was merely a convenient way to meet his needs. Although, for some reason, he did not like the thought of her sharing her relaxed principles with somebody else. He put it down to his eternal selfishness. Irrespective of their physical relationship, Baxter remained a strict taskmaster and Shilling was a dedicated student.

The workload had increased over the years, and now she worked well way past five in the evening, sometimes late into the night. Socrates would deliver her tray of dinner to the laboratory and often return to fetch it. On occasions, she would be so engrossed in her studies the food was left untouched.

He still watched Baxter like a hawk, but the tension between them had eased over time. This did not mean that he trusted Baxter, it only meant that Baxter had not put a foot wrong since their last altercation.

Baxter, on the other hand, was determined that he would never be humiliated by Socrates again and assured himself that the next time he would fight back. For now, though, he decided it was best not to cross him.

For Socrates, that would not be until one fateful afternoon when Shilling had become far too much of a temptation to ignore, but could still be abandoned at will.

She was a woman now. A maturity had developed in her, and the demanding precocious girl had evolved into a confident, commanding lady. She no longer used charm to persuade her peers, she now used facts. She had somehow, against all the odds, managed to earn the awe of her fellows and the respect of her professors.

Baxter would watch her debate a subject or present a theory with an ease and clarity that left little room for criticism. And if she was challenged and proved incorrect, she accepted it with grace, embracing it to use the opportunity and make an acquaintance with someone from whom she could learn. Though she had a strong character, she was generous, quick to laugh and had a gleam in her eye; in fact, she was just like Samuel.

It all began reasonably innocently when Baxter came into the laboratory late one summer evening. The sun was setting, and she was standing in the orange evening twilight that was still shining through the window. Her hair was tied in a knot, and he could make out her bare shoulders in her light summer dress. His eyes moved up to her delicate neck.

She was deep in thought and hadn't even acknowledged him yet. He walked across the room and stood behind her close enough that she could feel his breath. There was a moment when his conscience warned him of his impending mistake, but he ignored it. Instead, he moved, bent over and kissed her neck and then her shoulders. The response was contrary to what he expected, she turned around and kissed him fully on the mouth.

They tried to meet in different places throughout the day and night. Sometimes, it was in his lodgings or her bedroom. The old nursery had been ignored for many years, and nobody ever went into it until they did. The laboratory would do when they could find nowhere else. Even Annabelle's old suite didn't remain sacred.

Shilling was to receive news of her university degree on a cold December day. The Faculty of Science would be publishing a list of results at three o'clock that afternoon.

The university was full of hopeful students awaiting the ultimate feedback on their academic endeavours. The list was finally pinned to the noticeboard. Shilling fought through the crowd, eventually reaching the front.

Her eyes travelled down the list. The names were in alphabetical order. She reached the H's. *What? My name is not there.*

She felt her chest constrict and tears well in her eyes, but she remained stoic. As she turned to walk away, one of the students yelled:

"At the bottom, Miss Hudson! At the bottom of the page."

She turned and thrust herself to the front again. Her eyes skimmed down the list of eighty-nine students. Quite so, right at the bottom was her name, Alexandra Hudson. They had included her handwritten name at the end of the list, presumably an oversight, since she was the first woman to gain the qualification.

She felt euphoric and ran to where Baxter was standing.

"We've done it, Baxter, we've done it!"

She wanted to throw her arms around him and kiss him, but she daren't in full public view.

It was late, way past dinnertime. They asked the cab driver to stop a few hundred yards from the house so that they could walk and talk, perhaps more.

It was icy outside, and realistically, they could not risk being caught. They snuck into the coach house. It was dark, and hand in hand, they made for the steps to his lodgings. Once inside, there was no time to waste, they removed their clothes and dived under the blankets, freezing cold, to begin with, yet quickly warming up.

She lay in his arms, completely satisfied. It was a moment of utter bliss. The anxiety of the past months had taken its toll, and the relief of graduating engulfed her, creating a calmness she hadn't felt for years.

Shilling wanted to discuss the future. This is what she had waited for. She could now live her life on her own terms.

"I love you, Baxter."

Her tutor looked at her. *Oh, how I rue the day I took this post.*

"I love you too, Shilling," he replied mechanically, deciding to not meet her gaze.

"We have a future now. Don't you see?"

The elation over her results had not died down yet. Nor the thought of perhaps eloping with Baxter.

He got up and began dressing.

"Baxter, why are you so quiet." she frowned.

"Shilling, my contract ends tonight."

"What?"

"I am leaving—now," he said, looking directly at her.

"Where will we meet? When will I see you again?"

Baxter went into the next room and came back, heaving a suitcase.

"You wanted a degree, Shilling, and now you have one."

"I don't understand. What does this all mean?"

"I am telling you I am leaving."

He chose not to say her name.

"Where are you going?" she asked again.

"I am going home." he answered emphatically.

"Home?"

"Yes, in Dorset—home to my wife and son."

Baxter struggled to pick up the suitcase and left, closing the door behind him. He then lurched his way through the inner courtyard to the road.

Shilling leaned over towards the window and watched him disappear as big, stinging droplets of tears splashed down onto the window sill.

25

THE RETURN TO DORSET

The elation about her academic achievements had evaporated in an instant. *It is all over—he is gone. Or is he? Yes, he is married, yet I don't care. My determination always gets me what I want. We must be clever enough to make a plan together. We could run off to America, no one would know us. We have enough money to pay for his divorce. Oh, stop it Shilling, you silly girl, you have been duped like a fool betting his only shirt on a cheap magic trick down at the market.*

She was sitting upright, her mind processing the events. On the bed, incessantly, her grey-matter churned with options. She was suddenly aware of where she was. There was only a thin sheet around her, and she was cold. All the warmth from their union had faded. An overwhelming sense of loneliness crept over, thick and suffocating like the smog, then her body crumpled, and she leaned forward and cried.

The moment was surreal. Suddenly, coming out of her trance, she heard a coach arrive in the courtyard, and voices drifted in the breeze. Her parents had arrived home early. *Oh no!*

Too upset to notice they were not the first to arrive back, Shilling didn't hear the door open. Socrates let himself into the flat. He had seen Baxter Lee leaving, and he wanted to ensure that the flames in the grate had been put out correctly and that there was no risk of fire. *Hmm. That seems alright. It looks like he could do something right, after all.*

There was still a lamp burning near the bedroom. He walked over to it and began to turn it down, glancing around the room to see that the windows were closed. It was then in the gloom he noticed someone, a young woman, sitting on the bed, hair draped like curtains around her face. Her eyes and nose were running, and the sheet that was covering her naked body was wet from crying. To his horror, it was Shilling.

Ever practical, Socrates prepared to assist. *Now is not the time to ponder the specifics or question her values, it is time to spring into action. Look at her. What has that miscreant Lee done to leave her in such a sorry heap? I must try not to upset her further.*

Shilling was taken aback by the neutrality of his demeanour. It made her feel worse. *At least the intense loneliness is over, and foolish shame can take its place.*

"Good evening, Shilling. It is freezing in here. Let's get a blanket around you and warm you up."

He spoke to her most gently. In heartbroken short gasps, she said:

"Socrates, Papa is going to be so angry."

With that, she began to cry again.

"I will make some tea to warm you up. We don't need to rush to the house just yet. Your father will be tired after the journey, and there will be unpacking to do."

Socrates watched her in the dimmed lamplight. He could see she was utterly despondent. *This must have been going on for quite some time. I never did like that cad of a fellow.*

"Your Papa will be understanding. He may want to murder Mr Lee, though."

"Socrates, you can't tell him! Please!"

She was distraught, pleading with him, tears streaming down her beautiful face.

"I will not tell him, Shilling. You will. We try not to keep secrets from each other in this house."

"But that you found me like this, I am mortified."

"We all make mistakes, Miss. What do they say, 'to err is human'. I have known your father for many years. Trust him. It will soon blow over. You'll see."

He fetched the tea and gave it to her. She gratefully cupped it with both hands, and it began to warm her.

"Socrates, how do you know Papa will forgive me?" asked Shilling, desperate for assurance.

"Because he forgave me when I felt as lost and forlorn as you do now. There is no easy way to say this. I killed somebody by accident when I was very young. The case was in all the newspapers, everybody knew who I was and nobody would employ me. I applied for a job at your father's firm in Birmingham. I thought it was best, to tell the truth as he would have heard the story sooner or later. He said he could use a driver and valet. He gave me a chance when nobody else would, I owe him my life. I am sure the workhouse would have finished me off. I was at such a low ebb."

"Socrates, have you ever been in love?"

"Oh yes, Miss Shilling, yes. I know what sort of bother it can get you into," he said comfortingly.

Shilling got dressed while Socrates kept at a discrete distance, washing the cups in the room next door. When she called him in a few minutes later, she still looked dishevelled. Her face was pale but her cheeks still reddened with embarrassment.

"Socrates, when should I tell Papa the truth? I can't think there will ever be a good time to address it."

"My take on it, Miss? Do it as soon as you can. The dark thoughts will eat you up inside otherwise. A problem shared is a problem halved, and your father is a good and fair man who listens." he advised.

"Go and bathe, have a good night's sleep and tomorrow go and see him. It's so late, he'll think you're asleep. You'll feel better in the morning, I'm convinced of it."

Shilling, however, was anything but convinced.

"Oh, I nearly forgot with all this mess, Socrates. I was at the university today, I passed all my subjects, and I am going to graduate as an engineer. I am not sure if I will be allowed to the ceremony, but as long as I get the degree certificate, I don't care much. You know how I am with needless fuss."

"Oh lass," he said, a lump developing in his throat and tears in his eyes. "You've done it, against all the odds. Well done."

He knew how hard she had worked. He knew how much it must mean to her. She should have come home and celebrated, but instead, the joy of her stellar academic accomplishment had been stolen by that selfish bounder Baxter Lee.

Socrates escorted her through the house. They used the servant's staircase to get to the second floor to make sure they were not seen by her father. He made a fire and secured the grate, and the room started to warm up. He checked the windows and closed the curtains, then left her. Shilling put on her nightclothes. She felt like a small child again, in need of being looked after. Back in her own bed, snuggling under the covers, she felt warm and cocooned at last.

A little while later, Socrates came back to check on her and was pleased to see her a little less crushed.

"Goodnight, Shilling," he said soothingly. "I will see you in the morning. Get a good night's sleep."

"Goodnight, Socrates," she replied, knowing she wouldn't, but was grateful for another kind gesture.

She lay in the dark. Her mind wouldn't stop whirring. It all seemed like a dream. *How could I allow this to happen? Where is Baxter? Do I even care? Of course, I care! Although right now, I wish I didn't. Will I ever see him again? Do I want to? Perhaps, to give him a piece of my mind! Or maybe to convince him to be with me? Choose me over her?*

Oh, I don't know. It's all such a mess. How on earth am I to tell Papa?

In time, she fell into a restless slumber, and when she finally awoke at ten in the morning, it felt as if she had never slept a wink.

It was noon before Shilling dared to visit her father's study. He was as jovial as ever, which made her feel worse. Her shameful secret was burning a hole in her very soul.

When he saw her, he pushed his work aside, got up from his desk and hugged her. His affection was clearly sincere. *He doesn't know, does he? I bet that will change.*

"Shilling, I have so much to tell you, I have a few technical challenges that I need you to solve with that beautiful head of yours. But first, you must tell me your news."

"News?" she replied as the blood drained from her face.

"Yes, what happened at university yesterday?"

He said it with a broad smile, bursting with pride, anticipating glowing results. *Oh no! I am going to ruin one of his proudest moments.*

"Papa, I need to discuss something else with you first."

Her eyes were cast down, she could not bring herself to look at him.

Samuel was taken aback by her solemn manner.

"You look very sombre indeed," he said half-jokingly thinking she was playing with him about failing her examinations, but that soon changed to genuine concern. She was still his little girl to him in times of crisis.

"Papa—" She was so fragile she did not know how to tell him the story without crying. "If you're busy we can discuss it later," she said, hoping that he would say yes.

But Samuel wasn't busy, and he had excellent instincts when it came to his daughter's welfare. He looked at her closely. She was quiet and withdrawn. It was unusual for her to have no questions about his trip—no questions about anything in fact. What's more, she had not smiled once, looking a shadow of herself, crushed, and lost in thought. That seldom happened, and when it did, he correctly anticipated that her 'news' would be 'bad'.

"I have plenty of time today," he said, both to reassure, and to imply that she needed to hurry up and spit it out.

Silence won't fix it, my girl. Samuel sat down in his favourite chair, gesturing to the empty seat opposite.

"You can speak to me, Shilling about anything. You know I love you, don't you? Sit down, eh?"

His compassionate expression and her mounting guilt were compelling her to explain. *Just tell him. Come on, get it over with.* Despite making her mind up to speak, the words were still difficult to express.

"Papa, I've been having—an affair with—Baxter Lee—for the last six months."

There was a myriad of reasons why it was so difficult for her to say the words to confess her tale. This self-appointed woman of the world was tricked into a doomed relationship by a spineless, selfish disappointment of a fellow—a man who was already married. He had been handpicked by her father as a suitable tutor for her, not a lothario. *And I allowed myself to be easily manipulated with the word 'love'.*

Samuel did not respond in any way remaining silent and motionless. Shilling saw it as a tentative signal to continue.

"It—the affair—began earlier in the year, the first time when you and Annabelle were away in Birmingham."

She wasn't sure how much detail was necessary. She was about to begin speaking again when Samuel interrupted her.

"Why do you keep on referring to it as 'an affair', Shilling, if it was a romance, just say it was a romance. We all fall in love at some point in our lives."

"Papa, for me, it was a romance, but for Baxter, I am convinced it was an affair."

"Do you mean that he seduced but did not love you? Took advantage?"

He was confused.

"I am not sure, Papa. I thought his intentions were genuine, but it seems not."

"Where is he now?"

"He left last night, Papa."

Tears began to run down her face, and the sobbing robbed her of her voice briefly.

"—Because he returned to his wife and son in Dorset."

Samuel, who, as yet, had shown no strong emotion was now was overwhelmed with rage. Typically, an agreeable man, he was like a presumed-extinct volcano that erupted into an unexpected vision of hellfire and brimstone.

"So, you wilfully entered into a relationship with a man that you knew was married with a wife and child? He was never going to be suitable, was he, Shilling?" thundered Samuel.

"No, Papa. Truly, I was none the wiser at first!" she said in the most dignified manner that she could muster. "He kept it a secret and only told me about them last night before he left. He said his contract was over, and he was leaving. His bags were already packed, and then he was gone."

Fortunately, as quickly as Samuel became angry, so too, he became kind. *I always suspected that Baxter fellow fancied himself as a bit of a lady's man. Certainly, Socrates struggled to warm to him.*

Never one to crumble for long, Shilling had stopped crying. *I am never going to cry over a man ever again.* He reached over to squeeze her hand.

"My dear Shilling, love will make a fool of us all at some time in our lives. You are not unique." He smiled. "This is just a bump in the road that leads you to the love of your life."

Oh, how I wish I could make it better for her.

Shilling returned the squeeze with quite some force.

"Papa, I have more to tell you," for a moment Samuel anticipated the worst—that she was pregnant.

"I got my results at the university yesterday, I passed, and the graduation ceremony is in March. There was a frightful scramble as we all clamoured to see if our names appeared. Mine was at the end of the alphabetical list because I was a woman. I nearly fainted thinking after all that work, it was for nought! It took me a while to spot it! At first, I resigned myself to failure, but lo, there it was added in fountain pen at the end."

Imagining the fraught scene, Samuel put his head back and laughed that deep beautiful laugh that was so captivating. He hugged her again, this time with joy. She smiled for the first time that day.

"Oh Shilling, my angel, why didn't you tell me before? This is far more exciting than your unfortunate tangle with that Baxter Lee chap!"

The day that began as a disaster for Shilling ended in triumph. All the household gathered in the parlour that evening after dinner. Socrates had snacks prepared and opened the champagne. It was apt that they should celebrate with their staff. They too were the people who had cared for Shilling since she was a little girl, and he wanted them to share the good news. He knew they could appreciate what an achievement it was for a 'mere' woman to have succeeded in a man's world.

To mark the occasion, Samuel made a short speech.

"Today, our family is making history. As you
know, it is challenging for a woman to be
accepted into a university in this country, or
indeed the world. Against all the odds and with
monumental commitment, our Shilling has
passed her engineering degree and will graduate
at the end of March."

Everybody cheered, and hip-hip hoorayed, then beamed
broad smiles at each other, taking it in turns to hug their
young academic.

Socrates proudly raised his champagne flute and toasted:

"To Shilling!"

It was followed, somewhat humorously by a spontaneous rendition of 'For She's a Jolly Good Fellow'.

As their voices died down, Samuel called upon Shilling to
make a speech too.

She stood up confidently, with genuine affection displayed on her face.

"Today is a milestone for me," she said "and I am
proud that I can share this achievement with you.
I thank you all for always caring for me,
especially Lizzie, Socrates, and you cook. After my
visit to Wapping, I know what a joyless grind my
life would have been—assuming of course that I
avoided being smothered and sold to the
anatomists. Papa, thank you for enabling me to

take this unusual path for a woman. I appreciate the unique position I find myself in."

She gazed deeply into the eyes of each person as they were mentioned, and they felt the kind touch of her warm words wrap around their hearts.

"But the person I perhaps have to thank the most is Miss Annabelle. You saved me from certain death, nursed me and kept me alive in those precious first few hours. Thanks to the quick thinking of Papa, and Socrates, you were found just in time. Without your terrible misfortune and your sacrifice, walking away from the only life you knew, I would never have been here today. You have also brought love into my father's life, supporting him just as much as we all do. For that, I will be forever thankful."

Annabelle's eyes began to moisten with pride as a grateful Shilling hugged her till she could hardly breathe.

Samuel took a pace back from the little group. He counted the heads. *Yes, they are all here. It is almost twenty-one years since the night that we brought Shilling and Miss Annabelle home for the first time. Every person who was in the hallway is here now. We are very fortunate, indeed.*

26

THE MOVE TO BOOMING BIRMINGHAM

In the nineteenth century, Birmingham had continued to prosper into one of the most significant industrial cities in England. Hudson Forge and Engineering Works had been established for decades. The man who gave his name to the company did everything to ensure that he maintained an excellent reputation in business and in private.

Samuel was very young when he set up the company, yet he entered into the manufacturing industry with many modern ideas that accelerated his success.

With the aid of loyal staff and clients, he was now an industrial giant. Yes, there were challenges, some he had overcome, others he had not. However, he felt no bitterness or disappointment. In fact, it was all part of 'life's rich tapestry'. Sitting in his office, he reflected upon the 'old days' as he now could call them. *I have enjoyed a life far beyond what I had ever expected as a young farmer's lad.*

Samuel pondered appointing Shilling as general manager of the foundry partly for selfish reasons, regaining some free time. He had turned fifty-five in the summer of that year and still had a lively mind and good health. He had 'his Annabelle' who to him was always the most alluring woman in the world. Above all, he wanted to spend time with her, not be trapped behind a desk staring at drawings and balance sheets.

He had taken to spending more time at his country house near Birmingham where he and Annabelle enjoyed the peace and solitude of the countryside. Being closer to the forge provided welcome respite from continuous travel between London and Birmingham, as he prepared to take more of a back seat before Shilling took the helm.

Some staff from his Mayfair home had moved to support him at the country house, others with firm commitments in the city remained in London to look after the townhouse.

The railway had made travelling more comfortable than ever before. It inspired him to journey regularly and enjoy the splendours of his own country with the majestic highlands of Scotland as one of his favourite destinations.

With Annabelle's approval, they had chosen a beautiful little holiday house on the southern shores of Loch Lomond, close to the picturesque Balloch village with its imposing castle.

Though he wasn't getting any younger, Samuel still had big dreams. The bold idea came to him, one peaceful evening when they looked out onto the loch together as the sun began to sink out of view behind the imposing Trossachs. Samuel was always full of ambitious plans and would spend hours discussing them with his wife, permanently prefaced with:

"My angel, what do you think of this idea?"

She smiled. It was the umpteenth idea of the evening, let alone the day. His hunger for progress and success was still profoundly alluring.

"Do you have dreams, Annabelle?"

Despite seeking her opinion, he seemed totally lost in his own world. His face wore a frown and his eyes were darting about, yet not really looking at anything specific. She was puzzled by the vague but intriguing question. *Where is our conversation going this time?*

"Annabelle, the world is so full of wonders—Yes, we have been here and there, but there is still so much to see and do. Would it not be wonderful if we could go and visit all the things that we have only read about?"

"I love your endless plotting, Sam. You're never content to sit still, are you?" she laughed.

"I think it's time for me to retire, at least on a part-time basis," he confided. "I've been pondering it for a while, and I am finally ready to have some new adventures—with you."

"How are you going to manage it, Sam? John Green has retired, who will mentor your staff?"

He didn't answer her for a while, although secretly he had been planning the next stage for quite some time.

"Yes, that is the greatest concern, isn't it? They need strong leadership."

"I am guessing Baxter Lee is out of the picture?" chuckled Annabelle.

Samuel raised his eyebrows to indicate his exasperation at the suggestion, even though it was said in jest.

"I was thinking of appointing Shilling."

"Oh, Sam, it will cause a riot. She is a girl of twenty-one and has only just graduated. Do you really want to put her in charge of nearly one thousand men?" she sighed.

Oh, my love, you still refuse to accept your unique way of looking at the world. Alas, not everyone shares your progressive attitude.

"Annabelle, we both secretly knew that Shilling would run the forge eventually, else why bother to educate her? For the sake of mere vanity? I think not." said Samuel assertively.

"Yes, we did agree, but not at the age of twenty-one. She will be working with some men twice her age or more. She'll be hard-pressed to earn their respect, even if she performs miracles at that place."

"I started this business years ago with a fraction of the knowledge that Shilling has. I will ensure they toe the line."

"And how is she going to deal with these new trade unions that are springing up all over? They can be quite militant in their demands."

Tiring of the doom and gloom, he ended the discussion.

"The appointment will have its challenges, Annabelle, I appreciate that, but I am certain that she will introduce new refreshing ideas. We have to make way for bright young women. If the figures quoted in Hansard are to be believed, almost thirty per cent of women are business owners—and she won't be the first woman to run a factory. Why, just down the road in Dudley, Eliza Tinsley owns a chain and nail making foundry with four thousand employees."

Annabelle did not want to argue with him. It was evident that he had gathered enough facts to make up his mind.

"I am sure our foundry staff will continue to be courteous. We have always taken a little less for ourselves and paid them the best wages in the country. Shilling will be strict, but she will be fair. She has seen that model work first hand. I would like Socrates to keep his eye on her at first. How do you feel about losing him? I will ask him to report back if he senses any issues beginning to spiral out of control."

"I think it's a good idea. He is very loyal to you, Sam, and he has always looked after Shilling."

"Yes, I agree. I will discuss it with him in the morning."

"Well, now that we know what Shilling will be busy with, what are your plans for us?"

She smiled at him, Samuel still adored that smile, and he still adored his woman.

Turning his eyes away from the orangy-gold sky, he gave her an excited kiss then said with a mischievous grin:

"Annabelle, Paris was nothing. You and I are going to see lots of wonders in this world."

27

THERE WILL BE SOME CHANGES, MR ATHERTON

It would be an understatement to say that the staff at the forge were somewhat taken aback when it was rumoured that Samuel would announce Shilling the general manager—even with Eliza Tinsley as a local precedent. Her graduation was so rare, she was a talking point in the newspapers, and the workers had put two and two together.

The long-standing head foreman, Jim Atherton cornered Samuel in his office before the quarterly managers meeting. They had a good relationship and had worked together since the company was established all those years ago. Samuel respected his opinions and regularly sought his advice.

"Mr Hudson," began Jim "I am not saying it is a bad decision, but some of the men will be very unhappy taking orders from a woman."

"My wife was concerned about the same thing when I told her the news. Let them be worried. They will soon relax when they see how competent she is." replied Samuel. *Oh, for a world where merit should be the basis on which appointments are made, not purely if you are a wealthy man.*

"Obviously, you can't withdraw the appointment now that you have made it. The thing is, Miss Hudson has been in and out of here since she was a child, and these men don't see her as a leader, they see her as—well—a little girl. It's one big difference between her and Eliza, who took over in adulthood." counselled Jim with complete honesty.

"I know Jim, I know—but when did you last see my daughter?"

"Personally, about five years ago. These trade unionists are a tough bunch. Even I have difficulty working with some of the more belligerent leaders. They are full of entitlement, abuse and anger, even at as benevolent a workplace as this. I doubt that she has the strength to take them on, Sir."

"Jim, I think you will be amazed when you meet her again. As you know, she has graduated with a degree, and women in engineering positions aren't completely foreign anymore. She is going to require a lot of support. Please do your best to assist her."

"And the men? If they ask me questions about her, what should I tell them?"

"Tell them that she is one of the most qualified engineers that the university has ever produced and they have nothing to fear."

Samuel and his foreman sat in silence for a while, before he clarified what he meant to say.

"No, Jim, tell them this. Tell them that I was twenty-six when I started this company. Some of the chaps are still working here after all these years. Tell them that she is my daughter, and just as they trusted me to look after their best interests, they now need to trust her. They must know after all these years I would not do wrong by them?"

"I'll speak to them. Let us hope for the best."

Socrates delivered Shilling to the forge's courtyard at seven o'clock on a freezing Monday morning. She told her father that she wanted no welcoming fanfare and so, she was relieved to see that only Jim Atherton was there to meet her. She stepped from the carriage without assistance and walked over to where he was standing with all the confidence in the world.

Taking off her glove, she offered him her hand.

"Good morning, Mr Atherton."

She greeted him with a big smile.

"Miss Hudson," he nodded.

Although he was sceptical about her abilities, to spare her feelings, he made it seem he was delighted to see her.

"This is Socrates. He will be assisting me in a personal capacity. I believe you know each other."

"Yes, we do," they said in unison, then smiled as they shook hands.

Jim liked Socrates. He thought he was a good man.

"I have three crates to offload, Mr Atherton. Can I please borrow a few of our lads to assist Socrates?" she asked politely.

"Of course, Miss Hudson. You can call me, Jim."

He looked over at the carriage in preparation to assist. With an inquisitive tone, he queried the instruction.

"I don't mean to be rude, Shilling, but what is in them?"

She laughed out loud. That laugh's just like her father's. It seems the apple might not have fallen far from the tree after all.

"Don't be afraid, Jim. They are filled with books— lots and lots of engineering textbooks, in fact, not my most private of possessions."

He smiled at her tenacity.

After organising the move of the luggage, Jim took her upstairs to her new office, a sizeable corner room.

There was nothing architecturally beautiful inside. It was simple and functional. As Jim watched her surveying the office, he had to agree with Samuel that she was no longer the child he had last seen five years ago.

Now, she was calm, confident and commanding, though not rude or arrogant and her demeanour reminded Jim of the young Samuel. Her hair was pulled back severely from her face. The black eyebrows and eyelashes framed her emerald eyes.

He was a little surprised when she removed her coat. Underneath it, she was wearing simple workers clothes, a rough grey skirt, a dull grey blouse and sensible, flat, work boots.

Shilling was clearly committed to running the forge, and Jim appreciated her forthright manner.

"My father says that I can trust you to support me and advise me as I get settled in here."

"Yes, I have promised," answered Jim.

"I know that the major objections to my appointment as manager here are firstly that I am a meagre woman and secondly my tender young age."

She spoke the words with a playful smile. Her honesty and her understatement made Jim chortle.

"Yes, Miss Hudson, those are indeed the chief objections, for now. I am sure the lads could find some more with time." he joked, causing Shilling to give a humorous wince in response.

"Please don't tempt fate, Jim! Now, I want to make some improvements—"

"Such as?" Jim interrupted

"Well, there's electricity, to begin with," she confirmed.

Jim sighed at the magnitude of the change electrification required. There would be so many new things to learn and perfect. I can see *Shilling is going to make us all work hard. Perhaps it is time for me to retire too?*

"I am going to introduce several new technologies to modernise the forge. The government is introducing a new safety bill that will also mean further adaptations are required. There is so much we can do to improve our operation."

"I fear I know nothing about electricity, Shilling. It's like magic to an old steam-powered Luddite like me."

"Then let us find somebody who does, Jim. Am I allowed to suggest myself, for that role?" she grinned. "Oh, and can I please lead the morning address to all the men tomorrow. And I'll need a tour of the factory as well. Can you see to it, please?"

She gave him her tried and tested, dazzling, persuasive, smile.

"Yes, of course, Shilling."

She was so like Samuel that his faith in her was beginning to increase by the hour.

28

SHILLING'S FORMAL ADDRESS

Without the experienced hand of Socrates to steady her, Shilling would have been somewhat adrift in Birmingham. Not only could she trust him, but he was something reassuringly familiar in a foreign environment.

It was Tuesday morning, and she would be addressing the men at eleven o'clock. Jim, in his capacity as foreman, accompanied Shilling into the area where the meeting would be held.

Shilling had dressed smartly but severely. She had done her best to subtly look masculine in her choice of clothing. She was wearing a straight woollen black coat over a simple grey shirt that buttoned to her chin. Her skirt, barely padded out with petticoats, was plain black with no embellishments. It was gathered at the waist and hung to her ankles, looking more like wide-cut trousers, than a traditional women's skirt. Her hair was pulled back tightly to minimise the look of it. This unconventional guise was to become her regular attire at work.

Shilling prepared to walk onto the makeshift podium. She felt the elevated position would help accentuate her seniority. There were sniggers, jeers and whistles behind her back as she stepped up. *Whoever that was had no manners.* Looking stern, it was hard to tell if she was intimidated or furious. Jim mistook her expression as intimidated, saying:

> "Shilling, please don't be nervous, these men know your father, and they respect him."

> "I am not in the slightest bit afraid, Jim" she responded with determination flashing in her eyes, "and I have no intention of riding on the coattails of my father either."

Put firmly in his place, Jim thought it best not to say another word. Now standing above a sea of heads, she began her well-rehearsed speech.

> "Gentlemen, you are no doubt aware that I am the new general manager of Hudson Forge and Engineers."

The men shuffled restlessly, either not particular about paying attention or only listening in to find something to challenge her on behind her back. This was all very new to them, and they were torn between loyalty to her father, and the confusion of a new, female manager. *Whoever could have imagined such a thing at our forge?*

Reading their minds, images of Ada Lovelace, Mary Somerville, Caroline Herschel, Williamina Fleming and more flooded into her heart, filling her with confidence. *I am not the first trailblazer, no matter what they might think.*

"My father has run this company successfully for decades, and he has entrusted me to run it for many more. I know your objections regarding my appointment that I am young and that I am a woman. I will not reveal my academic credentials to justify myself to you. If your respect for me hinges on that detail, then you may approach Mr Atherton after the meeting who will be happy to assist."

She looked at the men, who still seemed utterly confused by the situation.

"We have a tradition in this family of looking after our workers. My father had your full respect from the moment he began this company, and you will treat me with the same respect, I am sure, irrespective of your objections you might have in these early days. There will be new developments with no risk of job losses."

"We've 'eard that all before. Look what 'appened at Buckingham's place. Scores of good 'ardworking men replaced by one new machine!" yelled an angry heckler.

Shilling continued, giving no sign the words had stung.

"Rather, we shall usher in a new era for the forge, keeping us at the forefront of our industry. This company will now resume business as usual— with me at the helm."

The men shuffled back to their stations. The speech was not what they had anticipated, and the lady was tougher than they had imagined her to be.

Shilling climbed off the podium and walked to her office, Jim followed dutifully, if a little disconcerted, behind her.

"Shilling, are you trying to make life difficult? Technological change is one of the union's biggest bugbears," he said, trying to be calm.

"No!" she replied assertively.

"Shilling, I could see that the men were— unhappy—with your plan for the future."

"Really? We have the biggest foundry with the best employment record, and we pay more than any other firm, am I correct, Jim?"

"Yes, but I know when they are disgruntled. What do you want me to say if they complain about you?"

Shilling was quiet for a while, staring at nothing. Then she turned her head and looked at her foreman.

"You can tell them this, Jim. You tell them that I am the boss, and the next time I address them, they will show me the relevant respect, if they don't follow that instruction they are free to leave. Furthermore, from this day onward they will all refer to me as Shilling, no more Miss Hudson nonsense."

After Jim left the office, a few minutes later, there was a knock on her door.

"Come in."

It was Socrates.

"Well it seems you don't need help with much, Shilling," he asked with a smile. "I just heard Jim on the factory floor awkwardly making the announcement about how you wanted to be addressed in future. Ever the rule breaker, aren't you." laughed Socrates.

Shilling also chuckled. It felt good to share a lighter moment with someone who was on her side.

"Socrates, I would like you to arrange accommodation for us at the Royal Victoria Hotel. It is too far to commute between the country house and the city, even if it is by train. I will also prefer to be available to the staff at any time of the day or night. With electric lighting, we can greatly extend working hours, if we so wish."

"I agree, Shilling. We can still go to the country for the weekends, but perhaps for the next few months it will be prudent to be based more locally."

"Thank you. Will you arrange our clothes to be dealt with once they arrive at the hotel. Lizzy is not terribly good at packing. I fear they may be rather crumpled."

Socrates gave a broad smile.

"Yes, there is that. Do you need anything here?

"I need a large blackboard, please. I am used to doing my scientific calculations that way. Can you please purchase one?"

"Thank you for prompting me to shop for you, but I meant more as moral support here, Shilling. I know you are a brilliant and accomplished woman, but your father has still given me strict instructions to tend to your wellbeing."

Shilling looked towards the floor, feeling overcome with a rare flash of shyness.

"Socrates, you have always looked after me."

"If you have any problems with the men, please tell me. I do not want you to suffer any form of hardship. You never do choose to follow the easy path."

"Nobody is going to hurt me, and words are simply words, not weapons."

She got a lump in her throat which was thankfully cleared with a light cough.

"In the unlikely event something might happen, Socrates, I will tell you. I promise."

With their impromptu meeting over, Shilling went off to follow Jim through the foundry. It was a dirty environment. The clanking noises were deafening. Sparks sprayed out like fireworks. Rivers of red-hot metal flooded out of crucibles and into the casting moulds. The workers were covered in black dust from the coal fires. They looked more like miners than foundry men. Shilling smiled with a mixture of awe and delight.

As she inspected different stations, examined various tools and got closer to the furnace area, she too also became covered in black soot. It did not bother her. In fact, she felt it might help her gain the men's support. *Who doesn't like a grafter?* She progressed through the rest of the factory, speaking to different supervisors as she went.

The most critical area was the blast furnace. Maintaining a constant high temperature was an eternal struggle in foundries. This was the area in which she was seeking to modernise the process after electrification of the lighting.

As she was discussing the temperature challenges with the supervisor, she was aware of movement to the right in the corner of her eye. She turned to see what it was and looked straight into the furtive eyes of a young boy. *He seems no more than seven if that!* She finished her conversation with the furnaceman and went back to her office.

On her way, she instructed Jim to come and see her.

"In private," she added.

Jim followed her in.

"Jim, you have worked for this company for a long time?"

"Yes, Shilling."

"Then please tell me what a child is doing on my forge floor?"

"Well, we thought that we would only need the boy as a sweeper and it is not enough work for a grown man."

Jim was unprepared for this conversation.

"Can you remind me, Jim, the law says a worker must be ten years of age and above, does it not?" asked Shilling, already fully aware of the answer.

"That is correct, Miss. We should not employ young children."

"You are lucky you are explaining this sorry tale to me and not the government's factory inspector! Does that child have a father at home?"

"Yes, Shilling, but he is an older gentleman and quite infirm these days after he was injured."

"Well, Jim, the answer seems quite simple. Get the man in here, give him the sweeping job and send his son home. I am sure moving a brush will not be too demanding. If I ever find another child under the age of ten on my factory floor, you will leave with him. Is that clear?"

"Yes, I understand. I am sorry about that. Thank you, Miss Shilling."

It was becoming clear who was wearing the metaphorical trousers at the forge.

29

THE BROKEN, BEATEN AND THE DAMNED

Shilling and Socrates moved into the sumptuous Royal Victoria Hotel that day. Without her knowledge, he had requested the largest and most luxurious suite in the hotel. He was amused to note it also had the most feminine décor. *She will adore that, I'm sure.*

Her rooms consisted of a comfortable parlour, a dining room, a bedroom and bathroom. It was decorated in detailed flowery wallpaper. There were a lot of bay windows, making it beautifully light inside. The hotel had been recently modernised and benefitted from plumbed-in running water. It was a delight for her to climb into a hot bath on her return and soak off the dirt. The factory workers had to be content with the nearby public baths. Having a WC and not having to rely on a chamber pot was also a blessing.

In the evenings, she and Socrates would make their way to the dining room. Sometimes afterwards she would sit in the lounge bar to listen to the string quartet or pianist. Other evenings if she was overwhelmed with work, she would remain in her suite and order room service. Socrates stayed in the room next to hers and was available day and night.

On Saturdays, it was routine for Shilling to catch up on all the latest scientific journals. She would put all her reading material into a satchel and head for the hotel conservatory. It was the most peaceful time of her week. She would find a comfortable seat and enjoy the sunlight streaming through the windows.

One morning, there was another person in the conservatory. The young woman possessed a striking beauty. Her hair was so immaculately straightened it gleamed. It matched her big dark brown eyes. She had a child with her, a little boy. He was about eighteen months old, toddling about touching everything within reach. The woman had a gentle laugh and spoke to him in a low, soothing voice.

Shilling watched them for a while, wondering if she would ever desire motherhood. Her reverie was broken when she heard a familiar voice.

"Kate! James! Oh, there you are!"

A tall man was walking toward the little boy, his face obscured by the large, potted, parlour palms.

The little lad looked up to the fellow with pure adoration, and so did the woman. Big hands lifted the child up. The boy screamed with delight as the man swung him around. The gentleman looked around the room to ensure his son's squeals weren't upsetting anybody. He was pleased to see the conservatory was empty—until he gazed upon Shilling—whence, he found himself staring right into her face.

Baxter was in a predicament, should he or shouldn't he introduce his wife to Shilling? Shilling was his most famous protégé. *I can't see a way to avoid it.* If Kate found out that this was Shilling Hudson and he had never made an introduction, she would be suspicious. *Rightly so.*

Baxter was still holding the child aloft, frozen with indecision. Regaining his composure, he walked toward Shilling, lowering and balancing his son on his arm with Kate following obediently behind, ready to leave.

"Hello, Miss Hudson," he said, giving her the biggest smile he could manage under the circumstances.

He shook her hand, holding it a second too long.

"Hello, Baxter." smiled Shilling through gritted teeth, understanding that she was supposed to comply with his polite little charade.

"Please allow me to introduce you. This is Shilling Hudson; and this is Kate Lee, my wife, and James, my son."

Kate was confident and well-spoken.

"Good morning, Miss. So, you are the student who kept my husband busy in London all those years?"

There was genuine good humour behind the question. *Baxter has clearly not mentioned the full facts to her.*

Though it was difficult, Shilling smiled. She felt that annoying lump in her throat again, and her smile was about to fail her. It took all her will to keep it in place.

"I am pleased to meet you, Mrs Lee."

It would do no good to hurt this woman. After all, she is also a victim of this rotter's philandering too.

"I am surprised to see you in Birmingham, Shilling."

"Perhaps you will also be amazed to know that I am the new general manager of Hudson Forge and Engineering?"

Kate re-entered the conversation.

"We must visit with each other. It would be delightful. Baxter is working for Sir Charles Buckingham. We are new to the area and have few friends here. At least the two of you can share an intelligent conversation about science. My husband thinks that I am terribly dull passing the time with my needlework," she said with a sincere smile.

"Thank you for the invitation, Mrs Lee," said Shilling. She seems pleasant enough. Under different *circumstances, I could have, perhaps befriended her.*

Baxter sighed with relief as he, Kate and his son, left the conservatory with his reputation intact. He was grateful that Shilling still cared enough to be discreet. He would thank her later.

Shilling sat down, all thoughts of reading the journals were cast aside. She realised how naïve she was to think that she would never see him again. If it wasn't Birmingham, it would have been one of the other sites of heavy industry. *The child, James, he looked almost two.* She did the calculations. He had started his affair with her at the same time, his poor unsuspecting wife became pregnant. *What a gentlemen Baxter Lee really is.* She picked up her satchel. Everything seemed to happen in slow motion now. She felt an awkward heaviness about her. Going back up to her suite, the peace of the day she had hoped had popped like a soap bubble. Feeling worse from the guilt of telling Socrates a little white lie that she had a migraine and wanted to be alone, she lay on the bed and cried.

30

THE DARK CLOUDS OF BUCKINGHAM STRIKE AGAIN

It was seven-thirty in the morning. Shilling was up bright and early checking her diary for the day. The offices were still quiet at this time, the clerks were not expected to arrive so early. The factory, however, was noisily running at full capacity. Socrates walked into her room without knocking. Shilling was surprised as he spoke, caught unawares.

"Shilling, I need to discuss something with you."

"How can I help you, Socrates? Do take a seat."

Socrates felt there wasn't time for that.

"Shilling," he spoke rapidly, wasting no time, "for the last two weeks I have seen chaps arrive at work badly beaten up, covered in cuts and bruises."

"Speak to Jim Atherton about it, he is the foreman," answered Shilling distractedly.

"No, Shilling, that won't help. I've had my ear to the ground, and it seems that our lads are being victimised—"

An impatient Shilling second-guessed what he was about to say.

"Are they being assaulted because they won't strike? Why would they want to strike, they have the best wages in the city, perhaps the country. We have never had issues with the unions. "

"Shilling, the unions aren't behind this. I have evidence it is some underhanded methods instigated by Sir Charles Buckingham."

"I see. Is Jim aware of it? Do we know what his game is, Socrates?"

"Regrettably, I think you need to talk to Sir Charles yourself, Shilling."

Concerned for the welfare of her men, she requested a visit from her trusty foreman—her other eyes and ears on the factory floor.

"Socrates is right," confirmed Jim sternly, "our lads aren't being clobbered by the union men."

"Who then, Jim?" asked Shilling

"We are pretty sure that the culprits are thugs paid by Sir Charles Buckingham. The lads are a bit afraid to say for sure, for fear of reprisals."

"I fail to see how Charles benefits from beating up our workers, Jim?"

"All he wants to do is intimidate our workforce. Remember that we have invested in more advanced machinery in our foundry. We have highly trained men operating it. So, if he can prevent these people from coming to work, it will take us weeks to train others. I don't need to tell you this is especially painful when we have our expensive machines sat idle. He wants to ruin our cash flow to close us down, Shilling. He is not happy with our higher wage rates, and word on the street is that he is telling everybody that we will ruin the cheap labour market for the other industrialists. Quite simply, we are paying our people too much. It's not the twee chocolate-box world of the Cadbury brothers here in the cut-throat Black Country."

Shilling didn't reply, she just shook her head and stared out of the window. She hadn't studied all those years to put up with these sorts of shenanigans. She was an engineer first and foremost and didn't appreciate the underhand pot shots Sir Charles was aiming at her workers.

Eventually, she spoke.

"Socrates, can we please go over to Sir Charles Buckingham's office?"

"Of course, Shilling, I'll get the cab."

Feeling like they were on a covert mission, they both sneaked undetected down one of the dark alleyways of the forge's 'goods inward' yard and on to their carriage parked nearby.

The streets were filthy with soot, and the sky was so black that it could have been night. Coal dust settled over everything, and the potholes in the streets looked as though they were filled with oil.

Everybody seemed to be in a rush. You could not distinguish men from women. The figures were simply shadows moving in the gloom. It didn't help that storm clouds filled the sky, and the light was dim.

Despite the distinct chill in the air, Shilling wore no hat. Her dark hair was pulled into a knot behind her neck and barely contrasted with the dark grey shirt she was wearing that day.

She helped herself out of the cab at the entrance to the building. After months in Birmingham, almost every worker knew that the woman with the dark hair and green eyes was Shilling Hudson. She needed no introduction when she arrived at the secretary's desk at Buckingham & Sons, which the locals called 'Buckingham & Sins'.

Shilling was escorted to Sir Buckingham's office. He looked very different to the man she saw in the foyer at Claridge's. The passage of time had not been a good friend to Charles. Over the years, he had put on weight, and his face was severely wrinkled. His fat, puffy eyes were like slits, and his bulbous nose was red from all the drink. His grey hair was dishevelled, and parts of it were stained yellow from tobacco smoke. However, it was the smirk on his face and how his eyes travelled up and down her form that repulsed her the most.

"Ah!" he said jovially. "If it isn't the beautiful, Miss Shilling Hudson."

"Good morning, Sir Buckingham."

"To what do I owe the pleasure, my dear? You have lived in Birmingham for all this time, and this is your first visit to my premises. I am honoured."

He lay back in his chair and looked at her disparagingly.

"I have a matter that needs to be discussed" she answered.

"Work or play?" he sniggered.

"Work," she said, taken aback by his boorish, suggestive manner.

Although stunned, Shilling didn't outwardly flinch. For an aristocrat, his office was remarkably dingy. Thick curtains clung to the windows. The overcast light that fought its way through the gap in the dense fabric got absorbed by the oak panelling. The tiny gas lamps that were lit around the room did almost no good. She mustered all her courage to continue, mindful of the lecherous atmosphere.

"I am here to ask you for help," said Shilling politely but confidently.

"Anything for you, my dear," he said, looking right into her eyes with a lewd grin.

He was staring at Shilling, not hearing a word she was saying. He focused on her chest area, desperately imagining what pert treats lay underneath her curious work outfit. Undeterred, Shilling stared back with a stern face that she hoped might turn Sir Charles into a block of stone, like a goddess in a Greek fable. *Sadly, that is not to be.*

"Sir, I would like you to accompany me to the union offices."

He was jolted into reality.

"What for?" he snarled.

"As I inferred, I have a problem with my workers, Sir," she said, trying her best to sound humble. "Certain union members are intimidating my staff on their way to work every day. They are being brutalised. They tell me they are accused of being no better than black legs and scabs. I know that you are a powerful man in this industry, and I am just a woman. I need you to help me find these vicious representatives and take the union to court for intimidation."

Sir Charles smiled broadly.

"Of course, I can help you, my dear. I am so glad that you have come directly to me."

He stood up and walked toward a cupboard. He opened it a poured some spirits into two glasses. He thrust one in front of Shilling.

"Oh yes, I have influence. Let me speak to some of my union contacts, I assure you, your men will be left alone."

Very clever, Miss Hudson. Yes, it is me intimidating your men on my orders. You have played your devious little hand very well. I shall simply lie to you and say I spoke to the senior representatives and had them see sense. I shall stop my cunning, little campaign—for now.

"Thank you, Sir," she said, doing her best to feign gratitude.

"I hear you staying locally at the Royal Victoria Hotel?"

It was no time for Shilling to drop the fake grateful demeanour.

"Yes, Sir, I am."

"Perhaps I can invite you to dinner one evening?" he enquired, clearly with ulterior motives as his tongue traced a route suggestively across his top lip.

"Oh yes, Sir Buckingham, that would be wonderful," she lied.

Shilling could not get out of the building fast enough. It started to rain as she ran to the cab. Socrates held the door open for her, and she climbed in with great haste.

"Shilling," he called down through the window, "are you alright?"

"No, but I will manage as always." she shouted back, "Let us get away from this horrible place."

Socrates knew instinctively she meant the horrible man and not the horrible, dour building.

31

REVIEWING THE DAY OVER DINNER

Shilling had her meal in her suite that evening, and Socrates joined her.

"Do you want to talk about Sir Charles, now?" he asked.

Shilling smiled as she told him how she had manipulated Sir Charles.

"You aren't just a scientist, Shilling."

"Why do you say that?" she laughed.

"Today, you became a politician too. I am sure the union will get wind of this and will go all out to prove it wasn't their men leading the violence. Somehow Buckingham will be exposed for the vile man he is and will be taken down a peg or two, without your name being tarnished for being vindictive. Your workers are no longer at risk of a beating. Well done Shilling!" he chuckled. "Your Papa would be proud of you."

Later, as she lay dozing in her soft, warm bed, reflecting on her earlier triumph, there was a quiet knock at her door. *Socrates must have forgotten to tell me something.* Shilling got out of bed, unlocked the door and opened it a little so that he wouldn't see her in her nightclothes. But it wasn't Socrates, it was Baxter Lee.

"What are you doing at my bedroom door?" she hissed at him.

"I have just finished dinner with Sir Charles Buckingham," he said quietly. "I needed to see you again."

Shilling's hair was loose, and it hung to her waist in wild curls. She looked flushed, sleepy, warm and clean. Her nightclothes were casual, a long shirt with buttons, the top few tantalisingly undone. At her throat was the emerald. Baxter recognised it instantly, and his mind reflected on his extra-curricular lessons back in London.

"I can't stand in the hallway. What if someone sees? Let me in." he begged.

She allowed him into the entrance hall of the suite but blocked the way to the sitting room. Eyeing the decorative wooden globe on wheels that doubled as a cocktail cabinet, he chanced his arm.

"Let's have a drink. We need to talk."

"No. I don't think so. Perhaps your wife might join you in one?" she said, clearly without giving it a second thought, which surprised him given the intensity of the physical feelings they used to share.

He put his hands in his pockets as his feet shuffled with the tension. He was so anxious that he could not stand still. He was scared he might try to touch her; such was the attraction he still felt.

Shilling watched him. He was such a good-looking man. *Please don't tempt me to make a difficult choice tonight, Baxter. If I succumb, it can only end with several broken hearts.*

"Please listen to me, Shilling, I had no choice. I had to go back to my family. If I was not married to Kate, it would have been you I would choose to be my wife. You do know that."

Baxter had a genuinely forlorn look on his face. Shilling didn't move. He walked toward her and touched her cheek.

"Your wife fell pregnant while you were having an affair with me, Baxter. Now, let me think. What could that mean about your calibre as a loyal husband?"

He didn't know where to look or what to say.

"I love you, Shilling, I always will. I have come here because it is you that I want. You with your fiery mind and determination. You truly are one of a kind."

But it was too late, and he knew it. He thought he could see her thinking about Kate and James, but in reality, she was pondering that final evening at his lodgings, how he strung her along until his last day, the day she was supposed to be celebrating, then waltzed off. Now, he was back assuming she could be picked up when he wanted or dropped like a hot potato.

She opened the door for him to leave.

"Shilling, I have made a terrible mistake, we love each other, I know it. We are soulmates. Can we please try again? Perhaps, I can divorce Kate? It grieves me to say it, but I find her so unenchanting, despite her being the mother of my child."

Stop talking, Baxter. I will not—must not—let you sway me.

"We could move to America; their heavy industry is flourishing. We'll easily find work. We can be together."

He was so emotional he couldn't look at her and delivered the last few lines of his monologue with his eyes tightly closed, hoping he could convince her to give him one last chance.

All Shilling could think about was her sleepless night, the evening he left her, pondering the same question herself, and deciding, then as now, it was not to be. She recalled the trusting face of Kate Lee in front of her, a woman who probably knew nothing about his philandering ways. Shilling did not want the description of homewrecker and scarlet woman on her conscience.

"I am sorry, Baxter. Whatever it was that we shared—it is over. Do I make myself clear?"

It seemed it was. A defeated Baxter Lee turned to leave without a word. Shilling went back to her bed and fell into a fitful, dreamless sleep.

32

THE NEWS FROM THE GRAPEVINE

With relief, Shilling noted that the intimidation ended immediately after her visit to Sir Charles and there were no more vicious reprisals upon her men. Jim Atherton didn't quite know how it had happened, but there was peace. He suspected, correctly, that his general manager had a hand in it somehow, but the details had him mystified.

His suspicions were confirmed, when the grapevine came up trumps. It turned out an elderly clerk at Buckingham's' office told his sister, who told her daughter, who then told her husband, a close friend of Jim's, that they saw Shilling at the office. The news had trickled down, confirming that the feisty young woman had confronted him. He was rather proud of her doggedness.

Samuel arrived in Birmingham the following afternoon. It was a very blustery day, and he wondered if it might rain.

"Shilling is going to be so surprised," smiled Annabelle.

They made their way across town and were now having tea in their suite at the Royal Victoria Hotel. Samuel had booked them in for three weeks and, as luck would have it, they managed to be placed next door to Shilling's rooms. Samuel smiled:

"I have sworn Socrates to secrecy."

"I know how much you have missed her, Sam. Her moving away has left quite a hole. I think we should spend more time here. Shilling has done a tremendous job by herself, but nobody can work endlessly without a break. And, of course, she needs the adoration of her Papa for a while."

"I agree, Miss Annabelle," said Samuel affectionately.

He stood up and walked towards where she was standing.

"I am looking forward to seeing the changes that she has made and to see how all this new technology works first hand. Some of it is as mystifying as a magic trick."

He took Annabelle into his arms.

"Have I told you that you are still the love of my life, Annabelle?" he said with a stunning smile.

"How can I forget?" she laughed, "You still tell me every day."

Quite rightly so, Annabelle. None of us know how long we have on this earth.

33

THE SOUND OF BROKEN GLASS

Things were not always plain sailing at the forge. One particularly bad day, by lunchtime a critical machine had broken. By tea time, some water had flooded part of the furnace room, the steam from which could have caused a terrifying explosion should it become trapped. Shilling refused to leave until all the issues were resolved. Days like those were long and nightmarish, and she was mentally and physically exhausted.

When she finally left, a filthy, black frost covered the pavements, and the puddles on the streets were beginning to freeze. The courtyard at the foundry was filled with black sludge, creating a treacherous surface to walk over. No matter how often it was cleaned, the muck soon returned.

Outside the cab, ominous smoke, fog and sleet lingered over the city. The street lamps were on but made little difference. In the industrial powerhouse that was Birmingham; however, bad weather would never interrupt the work. Through half-ajar wooden factory gates, she saw the black and grey figures doing their jobs despite the elements. Shilling couldn't help but empathise with them and their miserable lot in life. *I am so lucky not to be going back to a tenement block. I get a break from all this bleakness.*

She saw youngsters scurrying along in the shiny yet dismal streets, wishing she could build a machine to control the weather like Mr Tesla planned to. The cab came to a standstill on some black, grimy cobbles. Shilling looked out of the window and saw the sign of the glassworks. Socrates jumped from the driver's seat and came to her window.

"They are loading up some deliveries," he said to Shilling, "we can't turn around for a while, Miss. We'll just have to wait it out."

Socrates was covered from head to toe in an oilskin cape to insulate him from the weather.

"It is alright, Socrates. Not to worry. There is plenty of goings-on outside to keep me occupied."

Shilling heard the commotion at the loading dock. She was cold and bored, and her curiosity was getting the better of her. Climbing out of the cab, she went to stand next to Socrates. She could see the smoking chimneys and could feel the warmth of the furnaces radiating through the open doors even at a distance. Glass making was fascinating. *How they make those big fragile sheets is still a mystery.* It required incredible skill and workmanship, and she made a mental note to ask for a tour of the facility. It was a whole different world to that of iron and steel.

The loading dock was full of activity now, bordering on chaos. A supervisor was yelling orders at the top of his voice as the glass was carried to the wagons and laid upon the straw. The younger boys had problems balancing the long, thin transparent sheets properly as their arms were too short.

Shilling could feel anger well up inside her. This was a job for grown men. Four little lads were wobbling close by now, a sheet of glass precariously balanced between them. *The youngest boy can only be about eight years old.* They were almost at the cart, but the smallest child didn't see the frozen puddle of water before it was too late. He slipped, lost his balance, and let go of the glass.

It was too heavy for the others to hold up by themselves and the clear sheet shattered, the shards tumbling down like a crystal waterfall. It exploded into thousands of glinting fragments as it hit the cobbles. For a moment, everything stopped.

The nearby supervisor's eyes narrowed with rage, and his face took on the ferocity of an animal. The young boy began to scream when he saw the furious man coming toward him, armed with a thick prison warden's birch. He knew that was about to happen. Shilling was riveted to the spot. Socrates grabbed her arm and asked her to get her back to the cab. He wanted to protect her from the sight to come, but she twisted out of his grip. She saw the man bring the birch down upon the boy. The child was trying to crawl under the cart to get away from the man when he whipped him again. The bloody red welts on his back were easy to see, even from a distance. Now, the only sound on the street was the child screaming and the sickening thump as the animal hit him again.

Surely, someone will stop this brute of a man?

She felt a fury that began in her stomach and rose to her chest. Her heart began to beat faster, and she launched herself forward through the gawping crowd with Socrates close behind her.

She threw herself on top of the boy. The birch came down again, this time across her back rather than the squealing lad's. Thankfully, she had the protection of the thick woollen coat. It still stung, but much less than if it had struck the boy's skin through his thin little shirt.

Shilling turned around to see who the brute was. She looked directly into his face as he brought down the birch for the vicious last time. It hit the side of her face. She touched her head in shock but could feel no pain. It was only when she tried to sit upright to regain control of her senses that the man realised it wasn't any old factory worker he had just struck. *It was Shilling Hudson.*

Socrates ran towards her. She looked quite a sight. Blood was running down the thin, delicate torn skin on her face and dripping off the tip of her chin. He grabbed a large clean handkerchief from his pocket.

"Here! Hold this cloth against your head, Shilling,"

She was dazed and rolling her eyes in shock.

"Listen to me! Press this hard against your face."

Everything around them was like panic stations. The crowd had come alive. There was no time to fetch the police, but Socrates knew who the perpetrator was. It could wait.

"I feel about to faint," she said weakly.

"I must get you to the General Hospital. It's not far."

"I'm not going to a hospital, Socrates, take me to the hotel."

"You need a doctor, Shilling,"

"No, take me to the hotel!"

Socrates remembered that Samuel and Annabelle were probably at the Royal Victoria waiting for them. *Oh, dear God above, let Shilling be alright. If they see her like this, there will be hell to pay.*

"I can't take you through the foyer like this," he said to her, "I'll take you through the servant's entrance. I know where it is."

He picked her up and bundled her into the cab. The wound was beginning to sting, and the pain somehow brought her around. For Shilling, the ride was taking what seemed an eternity. The road was too bumpy, and the lights were too bright. The trip was a blur. Then she remembered the incident, she remembered the glass, and the child and the man. She remembered the birch coming down upon the child, but she couldn't remember it coming down upon her face, but it must have done.

The carriage charged into the courtyard of the hotel where the deliveries were made. Socrates went to help Shilling from the cab. He saw that her coat was soaked in blood. Taking it from her, he folded it inside out to hide the stains. Removing his oilskin, he put it around her. He put her hat on her head in an attempt to disguise the wound.

"Don't be afraid. Shilling, we will get you upstairs without creating a furore, trust me."

He was right. Hotel staff the world over were used to irate valets and footmen discreetly sneaking their drunken masters back to their rooms, though perhaps not injured young women. He asked for directions to the staff staircase. He did it so quickly and efficiently that in the busy kitchen nobody even noticed a battered and bruised Shilling climbing into the service lift.

They reached the fourth floor. There was nobody in the hallway. He passed a door and gave it three very hard knocks, then he whisked Shilling into her suite. Drawing on all her inner reserves, as she often had to do, she was now capable of walking and limped along to her bedroom, climbed up on the bed and lay flat on her back.

Dozing, she half-heard the familiar voice of her father, shouting:

"Socrates, where is she? What the hell has happened to her?"

Samuel thundered into the room, calling out her name. Socrates followed and behind him was Annabelle. Samuel was next to the bed, now frantic.

"What's happened, Socrates?"

"She was savagely thrashed with a birch by the thug of a delivery manager at the glassworks, Sir."

"But how?" he boomed.

"I am sure Socrates can explain later, my dear," said Annabelle trying to diffuse the situation.

"Shilling—" Socrates said, trying to remain calm. "Let me ease the cloth away from your face. We need to see what has happened."

He stooped over her as she let the handkerchief go. The congealing blood, now viscous and sticky pulled the tender flesh apart as he moved the fabric. She winced. As the fresh air touched the wound, it began to sting and then throb. Soon, it was bleeding again.

"Let me see!" demanded Samuel.

Socrates moved out of the way so that her concerned father could see the gory wound.

Shilling's face, the beautiful face he had gazed upon since the day he found her now had an ugly, angry narrow red slice in it, open from her temple to her jaw.

34

VISIBLE AND INVISIBLE WOUNDS

Samuel sat behind his desk at the Hudson Foundry and Engineering works. He looked at his daughter sitting across from him. How he loved the beautiful flowing hair and sparkling green eyes. Her skin was milk-white, and her smile was sincere. The slash down the side of her face had healed now, albeit not perfectly. Instead of her being ashamed of the defacement, she wore it like an emblem that reminded the world of the horrors of abuse and how she had stood up to it.

Shilling needed a month off work to recover. She probably needed less than that to be back to full strength, but she didn't want the men seeing her bandaged up after she had worked so hard to gain some authority. She stayed at the country house paying close attention to the condition of the wound.

Shilling remembered that years ago she had read about Lister and his experimentation with sterile wound dressing. She cleaned the injury twice a day with a diluted form of carbolic acid, and she boiled every bandage before she used it. No infection developed in the wound. Samuel was impressed enough to comment that, perhaps, she should have become a doctor like Elizabeth Garrett Anderson.

During her convalescence, she spent a lot of time talking to Annabelle about her future. They took long walks, and after all the trauma she had been through over the last few months, the fresh air and isolation were good for her.

"Annabelle, I need to find a way to help people by using the skills that I have," she said. "Papa has given me a fine education and opportunities beyond my wildest dreams. I do not want to waste that gift. I have realised that I need a greater purpose, a calling. I want to help the less fortunate. Yes, running the foundry has a part to play in that, but our men are well taken care of, there are thousands of people in this city who aren't. Like that poor lad who got beaten at the glassworks. Once fully rested, I am determined to return to Birmingham and do what I can."

Annabelle looked at her and wondered what on earth it could all mean.

Samuel suggested that Shilling find a small house in the leafy suburb of Edgbaston. She settled for a large detached cottage set back from the street. The furnishings were sparse, but that did not bother her. The bay windows made it light and airy in summer, and the stone fireplaces would be cosy in the winter.

Her bedroom and study looked out over a sizeable well-tended garden at the back where she could sit under the shade of the trees in summer if she wished. She was comfortable and happy in her own space, even if her father insisted she share it with Socrates and another one of his servants from the country house. She wanted nothing ostentatious. *How much could one person own?*

Shilling became obsessed with the back-to-back slums of Birmingham. The population explosion meant a lot of poor-quality houses had been literally 'thrown up', not 'built' in their thousands by unscrupulous property developers looking to fleece the workers. Her time spent travelling across the city meant she developed an acute awareness of what surrounded her, especially the hardships faced by the youngsters. She no longer lived in a pleasant little bubble-like she had done in Mayfair as a child.

There was a constant stream of deprived and destitute humanity that shuffled passed the forge every day. The homeless slept uneasily on the streets in the summertime, and they froze to death in the winter.

On a busy day, she chose to arrive at work at four o'clock in the morning when all was cloaked in darkness. Socrates would patiently escort her through the shadowy alleys that wove through the city like a maze.

She watched children in rags sleeping next to open fires, huddled together for warmth fighting about who would be in the middle.

The back-to-back housing sheltered entire families in three rooms, sometimes with up to ten in a dwelling. The very basics of heat and food were scarce, and hygiene was non-existent. To use the privy, they had to cross a filthy courtyard and swiftly kick the door first to see if it was being used by another tenant, or to scare away the rats. Sewage would seep everywhere if crooked landlords chose not to ask the night soil men to empty the midden regularly. Chickens and pigs roamed around the quagmire-like inner courtyards, adding to the mess.

On her journey to and from the forge, in her understated clothes, she would join throngs of workers going about their business, the fruits of their labours enriching the nation and the empire. Shilling found it empowering to experience the daily routine of the working class. It certainly made her not take her own good fortune for granted. She admired their commitment and application to their work, despite the never-ending terrible conditions.

Most days were still dark when people began to emerge from their humble, overcrowded shelters, the knocker-uppers banging on the doors at all hours. There were the older ones who looked frail, shuffling along, barely able to walk, to young children who managed to still be boisterous despite the perpetual gnawing hunger. Unless they were too ill or took their chances working from home for a pittance, everybody joined the cold, ravenous miserable throng on their way to work. How they still managed to be jolly living in such hardship was a constant conundrum for Shilling.

She was like a modern-day Henry Mayhew she read about in the newspaper, except she explored everything about Birmingham rather than London. She spoke to beggars and paupers about their experiences in the workhouse. She heard stories of families that were separated, children that were taken from their mothers to be put to work in the Manchester mills and the levels of terrifying abuse that were meted out by the staff.

Sexual abuse of boys and girls was prolific, despite the prudish rules people were supposed to live by. The torment of the mentally disturbed, the 'imbeciles', had no boundaries. As her interest deepened, she became more aware of newspaper articles and court cases related to these institutions.

On her first full day back at work, she had broached the subject with her father. If anyone understood about wanting to improve other people's standard of living, it was him.

"Papa, I have had time to think, and I would like to help these poor unfortunates in the slums around us."

"What have you in mind?" asked Samuel. He thought back to his early days trying to help by attending the ghastly Committee for Social Development and hoped it would be less fraught with difficulty these days.

"Papa, I am interested in teaching people skills. I believe that we can make a great social impact by introducing a well-managed educational facility for people who cannot fund their own instruction. They will also need help with better housing facilities if they are to concentrate."

Shilling sounded very serious. Samuel was paying close attention to her.

"I've made the calculations, and thanks to our efficiency improvements, if I use five per cent of the profit we are making on our exports to India alone, I can buy a building and convert it into a college. We can create living quarters, and we can set up some small industries where each apprentice can serve under a journeyman until they are qualified. The opportunity will be open to men and women. Anybody from the age of fourteen will be accepted. Even if we just teach them to better reading, writing and arithmetic skills or teach women the latest basic hygiene and child-care practices, it will make a big difference."

 "Shilling, if you undertake this education scheme of yours, I will need somebody to replace you here. It is going to be difficult to find somebody with your qualification. Have you got any suggestions?"

Shilling had already given this a lot of thought. She had even discussed it with Socrates and come up with a solution.

"Papa, I will not leave the engineering firm, I will remain with you. This is our flagship forge, and I am proud of it."

"So, who will run the college?" asked Samuel.

"Baxter Lee."

"No, Shilling, not that man," said Samuel showing his rarely exhibited wild side once more. "What on earth has come over you? Surely, you have not struck up a connection with him again?" he bawled.

Once in a rage, Samuel often struggled and failed, to keep his voice down.

"I am not having an affair—or a 'romance' with him if that's what you mean," she yelled back.

"Must I go and rake him up in Dorset for you?" asked Samuel.

"No, Papa, he is in Birmingham working for the awful Charles Buckingham."

Shilling was so angry with her father and his assumptions that she couldn't contain her fury for once. Someone would have to back down or walk away. Shilling decided to be responsible and chose the latter.

"Papa, you have become a monster about this. I refuse to speak to you any further about the matter until you have calmed down."

With that, she stood up and walked out of his office, slamming the door behind her.

It was the first time he had become the recipient of her full anger, and he was shocked that she had ended the conversation with such fervour.

Well, one thing is certain, she seems quite determined to make a difference.

35

THE QUESTIONABLE
APPOINTMENT

Like so many times before when he was feeling incensed, Samuel opened his door and yelled for Socrates.

"What has beset Shilling to suggest this man be the head of her college? Hasn't he done enough harm?"

"Sir, I do not like him either, but perhaps you should listen to Shilling's reasoning."

"Why are you supporting her point of view, Socrates? We both know that Lee fellow is a bit of a rogue, to say the least."

"Because she makes sense, Sir," replied Socrates.

"When did this knave arrive in town?"

"At least a year ago, Sir."

"How many times has Shilling seen him?"

"Once that I know of."

Samuel was annoying Socrates by putting him in an awkward position. Shilling was entitled to a private life, and as he protected Samuel's privacy, so he felt duty-bound to preserve hers as well.

"Where? How?"

"On a Saturday morning, some months go now, in the conservatory at the Royal Victoria Hotel Sir. He also introduced Shilling to his wife."

Well, this gets better and better! Samuel was still not satisfied. He tried to be less temperamental when he spoke to Annabelle.

"I don't know what has become of Shilling. She called me a monster today and stormed out of my office; then she dared to slam the door as she left," lamented Samuel. "She has never behaved this way before."

"Is this about, Baxter Lee?" asked Annabelle.

"How do you know? Does everybody keep secrets from me now?" he shouted.

"Samuel, I will also walk out if you yell at me, so stop that ugly tone immediately."

The thought of Annabelle walking out, even briefly, was unthinkable. He took a few minutes to compose himself. The thick red mist faded, and his rational, clear thinking returned.

"Why is she so besotted with the man?"

"She is not besotted with him at all. She wants to work at Hudson Forge with you. You have entrusted her to look after your company and appointed her the general manager when she was twenty-one, and she has done a sterling job. She wants to help people, Samuel. She is a perfectionist, and she believes that Baxter Lee is a highly qualified academic who has the relevant qualifications to run the college, whatever character faults he might have as a husband.

"Baxter Lee, the man, the—lothario?"

Annabelle thought there would never be a good time to divulge the next bit of information. *Oh, to hell with it, he needs to know.*

"She told me that he went to her room at the hotel late one evening."

Annabelle could see Samuel's jaw clenching like a vice as he tried to stop himself interrupting.

"Wait, Samuel. She said that when she looked at him, all that she could see was Kate Lee. She turned him away. She does not love him. She has a conscience. Stealing another woman's husband is not her style. Shilling is a strong woman, and you need to respect that. She is your daughter; you have raised her well. Have some faith in yourself, and her."

Samuel was still miserable.

"There is a conspiracy against me. Why is she not happy sticking to the world of the engineer and now trying to become a philanthropist? Her plans are so bold, she makes the Guinness family look like they don't care!" he mumbled.

Annabelle started to laugh.

"Oh Sam, I do love you but stop being such a curmudgeon. Just give Shilling a chance."

36

MEET ME AT THE BOTANICAL GARDENS

Socrates delivered a note to Baxter Lee asking him to meet Shilling at the tea room in the botanical gardens on Saturday morning at ten o'clock.

Baxter was taken aback by the invitation and allowed himself to hope that she had chosen to take him back. *It could never be a conventional relationship, could it? Realistically, I would probably never divorce Kate or lose James. I do love Kate like a man loves a comfortable chair, but Shilling is an object of lust that my heart cannot relinquish. Oh, how I have tried to convince her otherwise, but as yet I have failed miserably. Perhaps, today will be my lucky day with her? At least for a few hours.* He gave a lustful grin.

It was warm inside the glasshouse tea room, and Shilling lounged in a wicker chair. Baxter saw her first, and he stopped for a short while to watch her from a distance. He had not seen her properly since his failed late-night proposition at the hotel.

From where he stood, he could see her hair tied loosely behind her neck with those wild curls cascading down her back. She wore a straw boater hat with a wide brim, and it was unadorned except for a blue ribbon. She wore a blue cotton visiting dress, with some lace and piping around the collar and the sleeves. Her outfit was under-stated, and it served to accentuate her beauty. *She's wearing that emerald at her throat again. I must forget those afternoons.* He sidled up behind her.

"Good morning, Shilling."

She was surprised to hear his voice and turned around to see where he was standing.

"Baxter," she smiled

He couldn't take his eyes off the faint scar. He reached out and almost touched it. He looked into her eyes. *I wonder how she got it?* Realising he had been impolite, staring at the wound for too long, he added:

"You are still beautiful."

"Thank you," she said, holding his gaze.

They ordered a pot of tea for two.

"Baxter, before you convince yourself to believe that I am here for romantic reasons, I am not. I asked you here to offer you a teaching position."

Baxter felt his heart burst like a popped paper bag. The good news for Shilling was that he now paid more attention to her academic proposition.

Within thirty minutes, they had an agreement. She would provide the infrastructure, and he would manage the college. He was left with no doubt that there would never be any romance between them ever again.

Although they were both pleased with the arrangement, not everyone was when they saw the planning permission for the new premises materialise.

"Good God, man!" raged Sir Charles Buckingham in his private club, with some of the most prominent industrialists in the country sat around him.

"Who does Shilling Hudson think she is?" he continued. "She plans to build a college and a shelter for the blasted poor, and she has stolen Baxter Lee from me to run the damned place."

The four men sitting around the fireplace all nodded their agreement about how preposterous it was.

"She is educating these ragamuffins and pushing up the price of labour. Direct costs we have to swallow," said Lord Ellington.

"And there is the rumour that she is interested in this new combustion engine they are working on for vehicles. If they come to market, who will lease my three hundred horse-drawn omnibuses then?" remarked Henry De Mille.

"I heard that she wants to build the engines, and is seeing how they might tool up a production line once they get a licence to build them," said Sir Harold Rose.

"She has bought some old warehouses and plans to run the college from there. It is a massive area. She can educate a thousand people at a time." commented Henry Deal. "We need to get Samuel Hudson to come here and explain what the devil is going on. This daughter of his is making things very difficult for us."

It was Buckingham's turn to pipe up.

"You will never get Samuel Hudson into this room; he can be immensely awkward when he wants to be. The two of them are cut from the same cloth I am afraid."

"What are the unions saying about all this?" asked Rose.

"Well it is all to the benefit of the labourer, so they are not opposed to the measures," said a dismayed De Mille.

Buckingham added:

"The matter is settled then, gentlemen. We must act. Put a spanner in the works for Miss Hudson. The question is now, of course, how."

He fell silent for a moment as a devilish grin appeared on his face.

"I have a plan. Leave it with me, my good men. I will deal with this exasperating woman once and for all."

37

LOOKING FOR BACKING

Benjamin Fischer checked the time; it was eleven o'clock on a bright sunny morning. His diary confirmed that in fifteen minutes, he had a meeting with Samuel and his daughter Shilling Hudson.

He looked around the room to make sure that the area was impeccable. The Hudson's were industrial royalty. Benjamin's London office was situated in the heart of the city amidst all the other prestigious banking and insurance houses.

The building was impressive. His office displayed one of the most remarkable art and antique collections in the country. The thirty-six-year-old came from the most reputable family of private investors in Great Britain—making them the most sort after financiers in the country. They specialised in investing in the steel industry.

Samuel and Shilling stepped into the elegant office. His secretary greeted them formerly and escorted them to see him. The floor was ebony parquet, with the centre covered with a deep-pile royal blue oriental rug. The walls were snow white. The classic windows stretched from floor to ceiling. There were no fussy drapes, so rays of bright light streamed in, landing in a square pattern on the rug. There was a French Rococo table at the centre of the room, long enough to seat twenty people. Benjamin's desk, off to one side was from the time of Louis XIV, and all the artworks displayed on the walls were original. Shilling could identify a Rembrandt and a small Caravaggio before she thought it best to concentrate on the meeting.

Benjamin stood up and walked towards them.

"Hello Samuel," he said, shaking his hand. "I am delighted to see you again," he added with genuine affection.

"Benjamin," he replied, reverentially nodding his head with similar enthusiasm. "Please let me introduce my daughter Shilling to you."

"I am pleased to meet you, Miss Shilling."

Benjamin ordered tea, and they sat down at his desk, in three luxurious upholstered chairs. Shilling studied him carefully.

"How can I help you, Samuel?" asked the financier politely.

"Well, it is Shilling that needs your assistance—" Samuel paused. "Perhaps she can tell you about it."

Shilling began to speak at length about her plans for the combustion engine production line. After two minutes, Benjamin realised that he hadn't heard a word she said because he had just met the most beautiful woman in the world.

Everything about her was a delight. Her eyes were emerald green and matched the huge emerald at her throat. Her tamed curly hair framed her face beautifully. Her skin was pale and without a blemish, except for the faint scar along the side of her face. He wondered how she might have got it. *Perhaps it was a riding accident. A branch can create a long gouge like that.*

"Shilling, can you please explain the idea for your college again? It is many years since I did full-time study."

Shilling looked at him a little confused. "But, Benjamin, I was commenting on the plans for financing the combustion engines." she smiled.

Knowing the probable cause for Benjamin's absent-mindedness, Samuel was amused by the exchange. She began explaining, a little flustered as she noticed just how attractive the man across the desk was.

"There is currently a new technology being developed. It is the internal combustion engine. From what I have investigated, it will be a smaller, more portable machine that will be powered by different fuel and will not use coal or steam for propulsion. The rumour is that the German scientists are building on the work of Hugon and Lenoir, working towards creating this engine to propel a people-carrying vehicle. It will be called an automobile. It may take several years to develop fully. If this technology is successful, everybody will want one. I need the funds to start developing more sophisticated machines to manufacture these early engines."

Benjamin knew nothing about engines or automobiles. He didn't even research the subject—he simply agreed to give her whatever she asked for. The Hudson's had plenty of assets behind them, were they to default on the loan. With the immediate news of the secured funding, a triumphant Shilling returned to Birmingham within the week.

She was surprised at how she had missed her cottage. Socrates had remained behind, and he was ready to update her on all the news that had happened in her absence.

"Shilling, Charles Buckingham wants a meeting with you. He has left his calling card. "

"He came to my house, personally?"

"Yes," answered Socrates solemnly.

"How strange. I wonder what he is up to? Sir Charles only ever does things that further his own ends."

The next afternoon at three o'clock, a surprised Socrates announced that Charles was there to see her. He had turned up without setting a proper appointment. It was Sunday and a peculiar day to visit if it were a business matter. Socrates whispered:

"I smell a rat. Be careful."

As Socrates escorted him into the study Shilling got a whiff of the ghastly odour of stale cigar smoke. The aristocrat stepped forward to shake her hand.

Sir Charles rudely ushered Socrates away with a dismissive wave of his hand and closed the door behind him. Mulling over how she was going to handle the meeting; she did not hear Charles gently turn the key in the lock.

"Please sit down, Sir Buckingham."

She pointed to her three-seater sofa as the best place for him, then sat on her desk chair, as far away as possible.

"Call me Charles, please, dear. We are fellow industrialists, are we not?"

"Now, I believe you have been in London. Did you enjoy the trip?"

"Yes, I did, thank you," she replied politely. *Who snitched on me, I wonder?*

With the initial patronising pleasantries over, Sir Charles began his sly mission to deal with the 'Shilling' issue as he'd promised.

"You are probably speculating why I have come to see you today?"

He leaned back on the sofa, watching her.

"Yes, I only returned to Birmingham recently and I am not up to date with the latest news."

"Well, yes, of course." He stood up and started pacing.

Shilling felt her skin bristle as he got nearer.

"I have heard some interesting rumours at my private club. The word is that you are researching a new product, some sort of engine that doesn't use steam power?"

He waited for her to answer, but she did not reply. Getting nowhere, Sir Charles moved onto his next bone of contention.

"How is the college progressing, my dear?"

How does he know about that? Is there a mole in our midst?

"Very well, thank you."

"A lot of people are deeply unhappy about the college and are suggesting that we lobby to have it closed."

He was speaking confidently despite him getting no reaction from her.

Ominously smiling and speaking softly, he said:

"But I have a proposition that will resolve their objections. If we become partners, I will be able to stifle the dissenting voices. We will make such powerful allies."

He went to the window behind her chair, looking out over the beautiful garden.

"I am not looking for a business partner, Sir Charles."

"Oh no, my dear. I am not offering a commercial contract. It is a marriage contract I am proposing."

She felt him put his hands roughly on her shoulders. Trying to stand up, he pushed her back into the seat. One hand was then clasped tightly around where her throat met her shoulder and the other one gently caressing her neck.

"Just think about it, Shilling, you could have my children. What a business empire we could build."

"Take your hands off me," she warned, trying to pull herself free.

"Oh Shilling," he whispered into her ear as she caught a whiff of his stale breath. He slid his left hand through her hair and stroked her ear. Suddenly, he grabbed the tresses and yanked them sharply. Her head jerked back so that her face looked towards the ceiling. He traced the scar on her face.

"Oh, Shilling, you think that you are so much better than everybody else, don't you? But you are just a common girl really, with ideas above your station." His fingers moved past the emerald and toward her chest. He tried to slide his coarse fingers down behind the fabric of her bodice. For a brief moment, he succeeded. He felt her delicious soft young flesh and her heaving chest against his hand.

With one fast, frantic and furious move, she ripped his hands away.

"Socrates!"

Having wrestled herself free, she hurtled towards her study door and turned the handle. The lock kept it in place for a few precious seconds as Sir Charles looked at her scrabbling like a pretty caged songbird trying to escape. *She will learn her lesson and accept my offer.* She was still panicking and fumbling to turn the key in the lock. At last, the lock clicked, and as it did so, Shilling felt the door being pushed toward her from the other side.

The ever-protective Socrates grabbed Sir Charles and dragged him to the front door, whence he promptly threw him out. His smug air of superiority quickly evaporated as he tripped and landed on his hands and knees on the gravel pathway. Being too fat and inflexible to stand up by himself, his coachman had to help him.

Socrates slammed the door in his face and promptly returned to Shilling and made her a cup of tea. As she sipped at it, she explained everything. His eyes widened with shock as she recounted her experience.

A sense of loyalty made Socrates journey to the forge, whereupon he knocked on Samuel's office door. He was looking through some papers while the factory was quiet at the weekend.

Socrates hadn't wanted to leave Shilling on her own, but she had convinced him not to worry in her customary, respectful but forceful way. *Don't make a fuss Socrates, for heaven's sake.* That also meant he hadn't told her he was off to see her father, in case she tried to stop him. That would have definitely been labelled as a fuss.

To keep the peace, he pretended he was on a domestic errand. For once his loyalty boundaries blurred and Socrates could not withhold the unpleasant incident with Sir Charles from Samuel. *I have to tell him. Shilling was in real peril. Divulging this situation is more important than my ethics.* He gave a tentative knock at the door.

"Come in," announced Samuel from his desk.

"Good afternoon, Sir."

"Socrates. I am glad to see you; I have a few jobs I would like you to undertake this week. On Monday—"

"Sir, can that wait? There is something I need to tell you." interrupted Socrates sternly.

"What has happened?"

Samuel knew Socrates would never speak out of turn without good cause.

"Sir, it is Shilling."

"Is she alright?"

"I don't know, Sir," Socrates replied honestly. "She received a visit from Sir Charles Buckingham this afternoon. It had not been planned, but I fear it became an unwelcome encounter."

Unsure how to proceed, Socrates blundered ahead.

"Sir, I think he violated her."

Samuel sat upright.

"Violated? How?"

"Sir, Shilling did not want me to tell you, but something must be done. His base behaviour was thoroughly unacceptable."

"How so?"

"Buckingham went into Shilling's office under the pretence of an impromptu business meeting. He must have locked the door without her knowing it."

Samuel looked stunned. *Locking her in her own study. Can the man stoop any lower? What's his game?*

"Shilling said that he proposed marriage out of the blue. Of course, she refused. He put his hand around her throat on one side, as if to throttle her, and with the other hand, he reached down inside her bodice and he—he violated her, Sir."

Socrates saw Samuel's face turn red with rage. He continued.

"She was lucky to get away from him. She says she is unscathed, but I saw her throat is bruised and she is a little hoarse of voice. I sense her fear, Sir, but of course, she won't admit it."

Samuel's calm demeanour was betrayed by his flushed face. Still, he stared out of the window for quite some time, then turned around to speak.

"Socrates, find out where Sir Charles is, then come back and fetch me."

His loyal valet returned within the hour.

"Sir Charles is at his club, Sir. Perhaps he is in league with some other fellows? He might have reported back to them?"

"Take me there, please, Socrates."

"Yes, Sir."

Since Samuel had planned to work all day, he was wearing simple shirt and trousers, with no jacket, waistcoat or tie. He was in no state to enter a gentlemen's club, but he did not care. *Besides, these people are not gentlemen, so to hell with their rules.*

Despite not meeting the dress code, Samuel had no difficulty getting into the club. Determined, he elbowed past the dumbfounded concierge, and like a cannonball of anger flew up the stairs two steps at a time, with Socrates close at his heels.

The second door he tried revealed a sizeable dining room, with Sir Charles and his prominent industrialist friends, gorging themselves on a roast dinner. They all knew Samuel, but because he loathed socialising, they did not have much time for him and his aloof behaviour.

A dishevelled Samuel moved towards the massive oak dining table.

"Good day, Mr Hudson," said Lord Ellington. "I see you're not complying with the dress code for the club, old boy?"

An elderly butler had just arrived to serve more wine and now found himself wondering how best to evict the bristling scruffy-looking gentleman in front of him. Socrates caught the butler's eye and with the most subtle shake of his head motioned him to turn a blind eye.

"Well! What a surprise to see you here," greeted Sir Charles. "If I knew that a visit to your lovely daughter would get you to sit around the table with us so swiftly, I would have done it a long time ago."

The smug men around the table sniggered at Samuel, who by now was no longer enraged—he was murderous. He grabbed a heavy cast-iron poker from the stand by the fireplace and walked a couple of paces toward portly Sir Charles. Struggling to stand, he saved face by remaining seated at the head of the table, his hands placed authoritatively on top. He thought it made him authoritative, untouchable, like a king.

His nimbler friends backed away, sensing trouble was brewing. The nervous butler, stood like a statue, still clutching the expensive crystal decanter of the best Bordeaux hoping it didn't need to become a weapon.

"Now, think about what you are doing, Samuel. I will have you arrested," warned Sir Charles.

"I have thought about it."

Whipping the long poker against Sir Charles's hands, the bones crunched and cracked with the force of the blows. In torturous agony, Samuel's nemesis slumped back in his plush, red leather chair.

Socrates took a step forward to prevent Samuel from causing more harm, but his employer had achieved what he had wished and threw down the poker. He gripped Sir Charles by his lapels and pulled him so close, they were eye to eye. The odious Buckingham shrieked with pain. With his lightly-bloodied hands, he tried to struggle free, pushing against Samuel's arms, but the intense pain was overwhelming.

Socrates heard Samuel whisper a dire warning.

"Don't think of reporting me. Remember, I know rather a lot about you and your shady dealings over the years, let alone your deplorable conduct this afternoon, Charles. If you harm my child, I will kill you."

Even in his pain, the dire warning made Buckingham's skin crawl. Somehow, he knew that Samuel would do it if pushed.

38

THE BLOOD-SPLATTERED SHIRT

Shilling had decided a change of scene was in order and headed to her office at the forge. When she saw traces of blood on Samuel's white shirt sleeves on his return, coupled with Socrates's pressing need to run that spontaneous errand earlier, she had all the clues she needed to piece together the true run of events.

She got up from her desk and ran toward him.

"Oh Papa," she cried, "I can fight my own battles. You shouldn't have worried."

He smiled at her.

"Any loving father would have done the same, Shilling. It is the way men are made, I'm afraid. Sir Charles is a menace and the thought of him distressing you—well, it was deplorable. I love you, Shilling, always have and like it or not, it is still my job to protect you."

Reluctantly, Shilling dropped the matter and returned to her papers.

A week later, on a much more peaceful Sunday, Samuel was awake, but Annabelle was lying in his arms fast asleep. He looked at her serene face, her arm rested on his chest, and he smiled when he saw the wedding ring on her finger. At that moment, he felt he was the happiest man in the world with a lovely daughter, the most beautiful wife, thriving businesses and a wonderful lifestyle.

His thoughts moved to Shilling. He was still concerned, despite putting Sir Charles Buckingham in his place. She was so fiercely independent, and her experiences with the resistance at university and her dalliance with Baxter Lee had made her harder still. He felt her harsh reputation made her alienate potential suitors. *I know she is content with her life, but is contentment enough?*

He wanted her to meet someone special and fall madly in love, to experience the joy of a loving husband and children of her own. He believed that Shilling had given up on ever finding a spouse and that she would be quite happy to be one of those old maids. *Until it becomes legal to marry textbooks perhaps?* He smiled. *Will all that her life amounts to be her dedication to the smooth running of machines and the college. She will miss out on so much bliss.*

Annabelle awoke then lay quietly, her ear on his chest hearing his steady heartbeat, savouring the moment. He kissed her softly on the top of her head.

"Good morning, Miss Annabelle," he whispered.

"Morning, Mr Hudson"

"—Annabelle—do you think Shilling will ever have a love like ours?"

"What's brought this on, Sam?"

"I want her to be happy and find somebody who adores her the way I adore you."

'Mmm," smiled Annabelle, "that will be quite a challenge. She is very single-minded. Most men find that quite unattractive. They prefer the quieter, obedient sort, not words either of us would use to describe Shilling. Just remember, you can't force the issue, love makes its own decisions in its own time."

"I want someone who understands her and supports her, someone who is as strong as she is, but just as kind—but it seems like it will never happen?"

"Be patient, darling Sam. You of all people should know. You Hudson's are quite a contrarian lot." She squeezed his hand lovingly. "Remember, we lived under the same roof for eighteen years before we were brave enough to trust each other with our future happiness. She knows there is no immediate rush. Shilling will fall in love one day. She's had a lot on her mind and more than a few bumps in the road when it comes to finding the right man. She is young, pretty, and kind, and has lots of affection to give. It will happen, I'm sure, but as to when, well that's anyone's guess. One thing is for sure, it will be to her timetable, just like it was for you."

His wife had spoken. She had woven her magic wisdom into his mind, and he felt peaceful once more. *She's right. It will happen in its own good time. Let her be.*

39

HELPING THOSE LESS FORTUNATE

Every Friday, Shilling would visit the college to have a meeting with Baxter Lee. The vast warehouses had been transformed into a basic but welcoming learning environment. A garden was planted around the buildings providing a green space in an otherwise grey and black landscape. In the springtime, bulbs grew, and their colourful heads bobbed around in the breeze. It was never intended to be a beauty spot, but nevertheless, people admired its restful ambience. It was undoubtedly far prettier than a few straggly plants in pots in the tenement courtyards.

The building was painted bright white inside and was immaculately clean in the living areas. An adjoining shed had been purchased as a shelter where those workers down on their luck could sleep at night. They were little more than coffin beds, of course, but they provided a clean, safe, affordable place to stay for a large number of people. The carpentry students built the bed frames, and they took great pride in their achievement.

The most significant accomplishment was building indoor lavatories and washrooms. Indoor closets were becoming popular in the houses of the rich, and there was plenty of work having them fitted, a boon for the plumbing students.

"Baxter, what do you think about us training gardeners?" she asked him.

"I don't know if it is viable. Our college is bordering on an urban slum, we will need land."

"What are you considering?" he asked, always aware that when she mentioned something she had already decided to do it.

"I will buy a plot of land. We will provide the implements, build classrooms. We can work alongside the botanical gardens. It will work on the same principle as what we have here. We will provide a hostel. The produce that we grow can be used to feed our students and those in the shelter. We can also sell some in the city and use the profits to develop the location further. My father used to be a farmer in his youth. I am sure he will have some practical suggestions."

"When will we begin planning it?" he asked.

"Next Monday," she laughed, "when I receive the deed of sale for the land, with any luck."

Shilling had completed her work with Baxter for the day. She said goodbye to him at the front door of the building. On rare occasions, she secretly wanted to rush into his arms and feel them around her, enveloping her like they used to. Just in time, she always reminded herself that it was a desire born of loneliness, not of love.

A few weeks later, Shilling arrived at her office on a glorious sunny day. Looking radiant in her floral dress so unlike her usual sombre grey workwear, the flowers were like a rainbow of colour and the leaves the same colour as her eyes. She wore the emerald pendant at her throat, and she was breath-taking.

There was a knock at the door, and Samuel sauntered into her office. He looked particularly dapper this morning too.

"Good morning, Shilling, you look stunning." he smiled.

"Oh, Papa, you are biased."

He gave his customary charismatic laugh.

"I come here with good news, Shilling. Listen to this. We've been invited to an event at Buckingham Palace. It is an acknowledgement to the steel industry for their contribution to the country and the empire. From Queen Victoria's office no less. Look."

He waved the gold-embossed invite at her enthusiastically, moving it far too quickly for her to even attempt to read the wording.

"You know how I feel about the aristocracy and the government, Papa. Must I really be there?"

"I would have thought a woman in Victoria's position would have been one of your role models. What would you prefer to do, Shilling?" He laughed.

"Stay at home and read my textbooks. They never let me down, Papa."

Samuel chuckled again.

Since operations were going well, Samuel and Shilling decided that it would be good to take off the month of July and stay in London, tying in the gala dinner as well.

It was delightful to be back in her old bedroom, and she felt secure. She thought about moving back to London for part of the year now. Nothing was stopping her these days. She had responsible and capable employees at the forge and the college.

On her arrival, she was overjoyed to see all the staff. They still remembered the little abandoned girl who arrived years ago, and it was always a pleasure to hear what her next adventure would be.

The house was happy and noisy as everybody from the Birmingham household had come with Samuel. He wanted the full staff complement available, since, to everyone's amazement, he planned to do some entertaining. Socrates was particularly excited and resumed his old London role as if he had never left.

"Should we move back to London?" Samuel asked Shilling.

"I don't know Papa," she answered, "Do you think the managers in Birmingham can run the foundry without us?"

"Of course. They used to when you were younger, and I had to spend a lot more time here."

"But what will I do in London?" asked Shilling. "I know there is nothing specific to keep me in Birmingham full time, but the same is true here."

"Perhaps you should consider lecturing," suggested Sam.

"That is an interesting suggestion Papa, I will make enquiries. I noticed that mathematician, Mary Somerville, is to have a college named after her at Oxford. There might only be slight advancements, but they serve to remind me that I must press ahead with my dreams."

"And we can always be 'generous benefactors' to open doors, Shilling. It worked before," he grinned.

On Tuesday, Socrates drove Shilling to the university. She had made an appointment with the dean, Sir Michael Kendrick. The meeting had gone faster and better than she anticipated, so she asked Socrates to take her to the Natural History Museum in Kensington before they had to head home for dinner.

She was delighted that she had the time to relax and take time to study the exhibits. She hadn't been there since she was a student and there was an abundance of new things to see. She was particularly interested in the geological section. Socrates chose to visit the Darwin room, giving Shilling the chance to enjoy the peace of being left alone to explore.

As she walked into the room crammed full of exciting new exhibits, she heard a friendly, 'Hello.'

She turned around to see Benjamin Fischer.

"Benjamin," she said with a big smile.

Her hair was pulled away from her face, her white dress exposed her arms and shoulders, and she looked like an angel.

"Shilling, I am glad you are here. I promised myself that if I ever saw you again, I would sweep you up into my arms and take you home with me."

"I see. And why might that be?" she laughed demurely trying to diffuse the situation.

"Because you are very clever—and you are the most beautiful woman I have ever seen."

His sudden, intense sincerity confused her. Their last meeting had been a formal one to discuss investing in the forge. Shilling was in a predicament. If she went with him to his home, of course, it would be entirely unacceptable. However, her bohemian waywardness was getting the better of her, and for the first time in quite some time, she decided to be truly reckless. *To hell with it.*

"In that case, Benjamin. I accept."

A startled Benjamin Fischer couldn't believe his luck!

She took a walk through the museum looking for Socrates and eventually she found him looking at a collection of fossils.

"Socrates, Benjamin Fischer has invited me to his home."

"For dinner, I presume? What date will that be?" he asked.

"Today—now, in fact," she replied.

Reading between the lines, Socrates spoke in a low voice

"Are you ready for this Shilling?"

"I don't know? What do you think?"

Socrates smiled at her, "Shilling, the choice is yours. You are your own woman, and you have been alone for a long time. Perhaps you should move on from the long shadow of Mr Lee. I think you know your father will forgive any discreet liaisons if it is the right man."

"I am so afraid of being hurt again."

"I know, but remember you are more experienced now, not the poor young girl who was left crying on the bed by Baxter Lee. You can look after yourself."

"But Socrates, it is as if he has already chosen me. It's all very peculiar."

"I'll tell your father that you are safe."

"Thank you."

"Anything for you, Miss Shilling, anything. I shall wait outside for you at his house. You just give me the signal, and we can leave."

Benjamin's home was majestic. He explained that it was part of the family estate.

"But, it's like a museum, Shilling, not a home, I cannot imagine raising children here. It is too impersonal. Clinical even. You'd be terrified a floor got stained, or an ornament got smashed."

Shilling didn't agree in the slightest. *This place is enchanted.*

Benjamin's staff were like ghosts, you never saw them, but magic cups of tea appeared, and at dinner time they sat down to a beautifully prepared meal served by the same phantoms. It was quite a contrast to her experience at her father's Mayfair house.

Shilling looked at Benjamin again. He had attractive features with kind eyes and a strong, square jaw and a full mouth. He exuded masculinity in the way that only a confident man can. *This is a man who could achieve anything.*

At dinner, inevitably, the talk turned to what life might be like if they were together.

"I am a very private man, Shilling, I don't enjoy being in the social pages of the newspaper, I think you appreciate that," he said.

"Yes, I do" she agreed.

After dinner, feeling comfortable, Shilling had a private note passed down to Socrates telling him he could return to the townhouse.

They spent many hours talking. Benjamin was surprised and awed by Shilling. He had never met a woman with her level of passion and intelligence. *She is strong, yet strangely vulnerable, or perhaps honest is a better word?*

She told him about her charity work and the college, and about the developments, she was planning at the factory. She was a ball of enthusiasm that burned bright.

They were sitting alone on a luxurious red velvet sofa, the servants excused for the night. Shilling had never been alone in such a successful man's company. *Plus, he is attractive. A little too attractive? He certainly is easier on the eye than Sir Charles.*

Benjamin was an experienced lover. He undressed her one button at a time as though she was a precious gift, taking his time. He was passionate and intense, commanding even, and yet throughout she felt completely safe.

Shilling lusted for Benjamin before she loved him. Her long-forgotten bohemian streak was strengthening, and she decided to stay the whole night. She could feel her cold, bruised heart melting with each minute she spent with him.

After seeing her perfectly made bed and putting two and two together, over breakfast, Socrates refused to tell a grumpy Samuel where Shilling had stayed the night. The anxious father pushed his food around the plate, his appetite gone.

Socrates was blunt and addressed the elephant in the room.

"Sir, I do not divulge your private business to Shilling."

"I am her father," said an argumentative Samuel, his liberal fuse shortened after his daughter's experience with Sir Charles.

"I repeat. She is safe, and it is her business, not yours."

That was all he would say on the matter. A conciliatory Annabelle chose to support Socrates.

"We have discussed this, Samuel. Shilling is a grown-up. She will tell you in her own time."

Hearing the commotion, Shilling, just back from Benjamin's house, burst into the dining room.

"Papa, I am not going to tell you, so please stop pressing me."

Eventually, Samuel gave up and retired to his study.

Shilling hoped she would hear from Benjamin soon. She was not in the mood to be let down in love again.

40

THE INDUSTRIALISTS' GALA DINNER

At last, it was the night to honour the steel industry magnates for their contribution to the economy. It was to be quite an event. It was such an honour to know Queen Victoria had personally requested their attendance. Buckingham Palace was a glistening beacon of light against the dark London sky. Carriages were making their way through the gates, each one checked by the Household Guards on duty.

Samuel, Annabelle and Shilling sat in the cab waiting for their turn to enter. Socrates had taken extra care to polish the carriage to a flawless finish and to groom the horses to perfection. *Please don't let it rain.*

As their carriage stopped outside the entrance to the palace, the footmen came forward to open the doors of the coach.

They were announced as they entered the reception area. 'Mr. Samuel Hudson. Mrs Annabelle Hudson'. It was a white tie event, and Samuel looked gloriously elegant for once. *There will be no flapping shirttails tonight.* He and Annabelle made a beautiful couple.

Shilling, one pace behind, was the last to be announced. 'Miss Alexandra Hudson' they proclaimed. As she began to ascend the stairway, everybody stopped to stare at her. It wasn't often that Shilling Hudson made a public appearance and to the career socialites she was an enigma.

Shilling's hair was rolled into a French knot and affixed with her favourite butterfly clip. Her arms and shoulders were bare and revealed her ivory skin. On her wrist, she wore a dazzling emerald bracelet her father had bought for her, especially for that evening.

The emerald theme continued with her dark green evening gown embroidered with pale green beads and crystals that glittered in the light, making her seem ethereal. The hemline was trimmed with decorative black lace. The ensemble matched her eyes and accentuated her hair. It all detracted from the faint scar along her face.

Shilling accepted a glass of champagne, served in a delicate crystal flute, and studied the crowd. There were millionaires galore—steel barons, the aristocracy, bankers and, thanks to Victoria's extended family, lots of royals.

At the very far end of the room, Queen Victoria was holding court. She had been missing for so many years, following the death of poor Prince Albert, and Shilling was pleased to see her.

She caught a glimpse of the prime minister, William Gladstone, and several other prominent MPs. Sir Charles Buckingham was absent. She overheard someone say that he could not attend because he was recovering from a terrible accident which had left him somewhat incapacitated. Shilling was not sad for a second that the brute was absent. As quick as it appeared, she brushed aside the thought of the blood on her father's shirt that had mysteriously appeared on the afternoon of Charles's unwelcome visit.

The event was spectacular. Crystal and silver adorned the mantlepieces. Paintings by the most famous artists lined the wall. Van Dyke, Reynolds, Turner, Constable, Lely, they were all on display. Trestles loaded with food and drink creaked under the strain. Shilling nervously played with the bracelet on her arm. *The total value of the jewellery in this room must add up to millions of pounds.*

Queen Victoria would not make any formal address tonight, she was there as the host only. The Prime Minister, however, took the chance to eulogise, lauding the British Industrial Complex as the most potent economic powerhouse in the world, as everyone impatiently awaited the dessert course.

"What time can we go home?" whispered a bored Samuel.

"After the queen leaves," Annabel replied.

Hating enforced socialising, Samuel pulled a face. *That feels like an eternity away. I hope she is feeling tired.*

They had dined on the most exotic imported food. The salmon was from Norway, the champagne from France, the lamb from New Zealand, and finally beef from Argentina. Apparently, that was the tip of the iceberg of the gastronomic delights they enjoyed that night.

After the final toast signalling the end of the formal meal, they socialised.

The Prime Minister came to greet Samuel.

"Good evening, Mr Hudson," he said in very proper English.

"Prime Minister."

"It has been a positively splendid evening," said Gladstone.

"Yes, indeed" Samuel replied, doing his best to fake cheeriness. It could have been worse. Sir Charles could have been here, I suppose.

Gladstone continued.

"Yes, we have a very successful steel industry here in Britain. The men in our country are employed and have jobs, the years of economic hardship are behind us," said Gladstone, sounding like the king of polite conversation.

"I beg to differ," said Shilling, her voice crystal clear.

"Oh, hello, and what is your name, my dear? What were you saying?"

She was being patronised and lied to, and it irked her.

"My name is Shilling Hudson, and I beg to differ with your statement."

People were watching and the room hushed.

"There is nothing noble about this country's industrial success. As John Stuart Mill points out, it is built on the backs of hardworking, unappreciated men, women and children, most of whom have been denied a voice. Running on a system of brutality and greed, many have become rich by keeping their workers barely above the bread line. They are housed in buildings unfit for animals, and they die on the streets of disease, cold and hunger. No, Sir, you do not have an industrial success, you have a social disaster at hand. How rich do these men around us want to be? Look at the amount of food and drink tonight and examine the wastage. You could be feeding the whole of Wapping on what will be discarded tonight. Your schools for commoners are still appalling and the workhouses a disgrace. Prime Minister, we cannot deem a system successful if it can't benefit our entire society."

Shilling's eyes flashed. She was so tired of the lies and hypocrisy. This beautiful woman with the battle scar was furious, and she was telling the whole world.

The room was silent. The people crowded around Shilling to hear her speech. Gladstone did not utter a sound.

Only three people clapped afterwards, Samuel, Annabelle and Benjamin Fischer.

Samuel walked towards Shilling and put his arms around her in full view of the room.

"So, it seems you do know what true poverty means."

"Thank you for your support, Papa," she smiled and kissed him on the cheek.

Feeling the eyes of the room boring into her, she made her way to the balcony to get some fresh air. *Before they evict me, no doubt.*

Lord Ellington ignored the fact that she seemed to need some time alone and brazenly stepped up towards her.

"Certain people are saying that you have thrown a hand grenade into the steel industry with the college you opened, giving people ideas above their station. Do you have a comment?"

"Yes," said Shilling, "Tell Sir Charles Buckingham and his selfish, privileged little clique to go to hell."

She stood on the balcony overlooking the city, feeling tired, but at peace. She had no fear of the repercussions of her speech. Everything she had said was true. She just wanted to go home.

She heard footsteps behind her again, and she turned around to see who it was, hoping it might be her father.

It was Benjamin, his face strangely blank for once. She hadn't heard him clap after her outburst and had no idea how he felt.

He checked no one was looking, then took her face in his hands and he kissed her lightly.

"I am going to marry you, Shilling. You are the bravest woman that I have ever met, and I love you."

Speechless, her emotions tossed about like a fishing boat in a rough sea, Shilling hoped a gentle nod and smile would suffice for now.

Mrs Fischer. Surprisingly, I rather like the sound of that.

41

THE FRANTIC WAIT

Samuel was agitated with worry. When it came to motherhood, all that he could see in his mind's eye were Catherine Franco and Clare Byrne lying dead in sickening pools of blood.

He was not prepared to suffer another home birth and had been pacing the hospital corridor for six hours now. There was still no news of when the baby would arrive. *Heaven help me if we get to sixteen hours.*

Benjamin was with Shilling, holding her hand tightly. He insisted that he be at the birth of his child.

"Sir," said Socrates kindly, "Shilling is going to get through this, don't be afraid."

"What will I do if she dies?" Samuel had tears in his eyes.

Annabelle put her arms around him and held him tightly.

The door to the maternity wing opened, and Benjamin came out.

"Sam, the doctor says the baby will be here in the next ten minutes."

Samuel remembered the short, painful visit he had before Catherine was taken from him. He wanted to cry. He was powerless. He loved his wild woman of a daughter and always wanted to protect her as if she were still that tiny child pulled from Maggie Carrott's coat. Right now, he wanted to do more than protect her—he wanted to keep her alive.

Annabelle whispered:

"Benjamin has found the best hospital he could for Shilling to curb your fears. I know it doesn't mean much since you thought you had hired 'the best' for Catherine, but there have been a lot of medical advancements in the past thirty years. She will be fine. She will."

Socrates put his hand on Samuel's shoulder, Shilling's screams drifting from the maternity wing and filling the air menacingly. He was going mad. *It is just like he was hearing Catherine.* Inside, he was terrified. His head was swirling. His mouth was dry. He wanted to stay and yet run away and never stop.

Annabelle held him close. She whispered in his ear.

"Try and relax, dear. You are going to be a
Grandpapa. I promise."

He heard a terrible long groaning and another scream of
agony. Then it was deathly quiet. Samuel panicked. The
seconds felt like hours. Then he listened to the silence as
it swapped to a different sound, the cry of a new-born
baby.

Samuel put his head down and wept with relief. At least
one of them had survived.

Benjamin had insisted that Samuel be the first to see the
baby. He opened the door.

"Come, Sam," he said gently. "Shilling has a
beautiful granddaughter she wants to show you."

Samuel rushed to his daughter's side. She looked tired
but happy.

"Shilling, are you alright?"

"I'm fine, Papa, but I am worried about you. You
look more exhausted than me," she smiled.

Benjamin took the small bundle of delight from Shilling
and put her into Samuel's arms. A little woollen shawl
kept her warm.

"Look, it's a perfect little girl."

Once more, Samuel parted the fabric a little to have a better view of the infant. Her tiny eyes were firmly shut. Her one visible hand, aloft, forming a tight little fist. *I bet she's got that trait from her mother.*

Samuel was too emotional to speak. He looked at the perfect little face, and he remembered the day he found Shilling. It was the same day he found Annabelle. *What joy is this little person going to bring to us?*

"What are you going to name her?" asked Samuel.

"Anabelle Alexandra Fischer," smiled Benjamin.

Samuel beckoned his son-in-law and gently gave the baby back to him.

He opened the door into the corridor. Annabelle and Socrates rushed towards him.

"And? What is her name?" they said in unison.

"They have chosen Annabelle Alexandra Fischer."

He put his head back and laughed:

"—But I am going to call her Tanner."

THE LOST GIRL'S BEACON OF HOPE

Follow the story of Tanner in "The Lost Girl's Beacon of Hope", the emotional sequel to Forging the Shilling Girl. Can there be triumph over hardship?

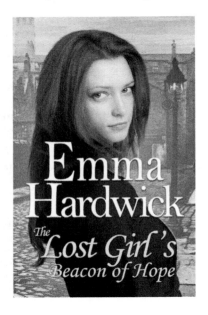

Annabelle, 'Tanner', daughter of trailblazing Alexandra 'Shilling' Hudson, abandons the family engineering business and plans to defend the working classes with her words. But she wasn't prepared for the horrors that she encountered in her crusade for justice.

In the heart of Victorian Manchester, a cruel mill accident robs young Emmy Sterling and her sister of their beloved mother, leaving them poverty-stricken and at the mercy of their violent, errant father.

Over time, their father's anger turns into abuse, forcing the elder sister to suffer an 'unspeakable horror'.

When Tanner learns of the harrowing existence of the working class in the industrial North, she feels compelled to act—whatever the personal cost. The bereaved girl's story about what she endured must be told.

But can the grim truth ever be uncovered if Annabelle has to sacrifice her own happiness and give up the man she loves to save the girl?

Follow this heartwarming Victorian historical romance saga about an ambitious young woman determined to use her own struggle to be heard in a man's world. Join her as she fights injustice in the lives of the impoverished working-class women struggling to survive in the brutal cotton mills and slums of Northern England.

Get your copy now.

GET THREE FREE AND EXCLUSIVE EMMA HARDWICK OFFERS

Hi! Emma here. For me, the most rewarding thing about writing books is building a relationship with my readers and it's a true pleasure to share my experiences with you.

From time to time, I write little newsletters with short snippets I discover as I research my Victorian historical romances, details that don't make it into my books.

In addition, I also talk about how writing my next release is progressing, plus news about special reader offers and competitions.

I'll include all these freebies if you join my newsletter:

- A copy of my introductory novella, The Pit Lad's Mother.
- A copy of my introductory short story, The Photographer's Girl.
- A free copy of my Victorian curiosities, a collection of newspaper snippets I have collated over the years that have inspired many of the scenes in my books.

These are all exclusive to my mailing list—you can't get them anywhere else. You can grab your free books on BookFunnel, by signing up here:

- https://rebrand.ly/eh-free

ENJOYED THIS BOOK? YOU CAN MAKE A BIG DIFFERENCE

Reviews are the most powerful tools in my arsenal when it comes to getting attention for my books. Much as I'd like to, I don't have the financial muscle of a New York publisher. I can't take out full page ads in the newspaper or put posters on the subway, or appear on a prime time chat show.

(Not yet, anyway).

But I do have something much more powerful and effective than that, and it's something that those publishers would kill to get their hands on - avid readers who are loyal and supportive.

Honest reviews of my books help bring them to the attention of others who will enjoy them. If you've got something to share about this book I would be very grateful if you could spend just a minute or two leaving a review (it can be as short as you like) on the book's Amazon page. On Kindle just click a link or scan the QR code.

UK — US — AU — CA — DE — ES — FR — IT

I really appreciate your feedback. It helps me improve my books.

If you'd like be a member of my 'Book Squad' and be an advance reviewer of my books before they are launched, you can find out more on the next page.

CAN YOU HELP ME WITH MY NEXT BOOK?

Like the chance to read my stuff before it hits Amazon? Read on. One of the best things I did last year was set up Emma's 'Book Squad'. It is critically important to get reviews on new books as soon as they launch. You probably weigh reviews highly when making a decision whether to try a new author or rely on an old favourite - I know that I do. Apart from helping to persuade people to give a new writer a shot, reviews help drive early sales which, in turn, means that Amazon takes notice and starts to tell more people about my books so more people can enjoy them.

To make that happen I have a small team of 'advance readers'. It's pretty simple and is, I hope, good fun. It involves them being sent a copy of whatever book I've just finished and then, when it is published, firing up a quick and honest review. Simple as that. Some members of the team have picked up errors that I've been able to correct and others have suggested changes to the plot that I have incorporated.

Apart from getting a copy of the latest book before anyone else, I try to say thanks with some exclusive competitions. In some circumstances, I offer signed print editions, else things like limited edition mugs. I try to keep the team relatively compact. There are a couple of vacancies at the moment and if you would like to get involved, please let me know. You can apply here:

https://bit.ly/EH-ST

ABOUT THE AUTHOR

Emma Hardwick is the author of several series of Victorian historical saga romances. She lives in London with her husband, and dogs and makes her online home at:

- www.emmahardwick.co.uk

You can connect with Emma on Facebook at :

- www.facebook.com/emmahardwickauthor

If the mood takes you, you can send her an email at:

- hello@emmahardwick.co.uk

ALSO BY EMMA HARDWICK

Here's a full set of all my historical romance series. You can also <u>view all my books on my Amazon page</u>.

The Hudson Family Saga

Set in Victorian England, two heartrending tales of torment, struggle, and love that follow the Hudsons between 1849 up to the late 1890s. Join the heroines, determined to fight for their own independence and success, no matter what grave betrayals, hardships and catastrophes befall them.

See all books in the series

- https://rebrand.ly/HFSaga

The Victorian Runaway Girls

Join these tenacious Victorian women as they strive to break from their bleak past and bring true love into their future. Whether abandoned, forgotten, or mistreated, each of the women has a reason to flee and never return.

See all books in the series

- https://rebrand.ly/RGSaga

The Victorian Sisters Saga

Two sisters. Two very different lives. In the Victorian era, fate can be cruel or fate can be kind. Which sister will thrive and who will be doomed—and why?

See all books in the series

- https://rebrand.ly/SSSaga

The Victorian Sisters Saga

Two sisters. Two very different lives. In the Victorian era, fate can be cruel or fate can be kind. Which sister will thrive and who will be doomed—and why?

See all books in the series

- https://rebrand.ly/SSSaga

The Victorian Christmas Chronicles

Get into the festive spirit and join these vivacious, strong Victorian lasses fighting for a brighter future, despite many cruel obstacles in these feel-good tales of courage and determination, each with a wonderful yuletide backdrop.

See all books in the series

- https://rebrand.ly/CCSaga

Printed in Great Britain
by Amazon

80249585R00181